Jim began looking around to see if he could orient himself, for even if he could get free of the restraints, could he get out of the cellar? Where was the door? Was the door locked, or barred from the outside? It was just too dark for him to tell. Then, quite unexpectedly, the door opened, and a silver splash of moonlight spilled down inside.

"Tyson?" Jim called. "Tyson, is that you?"

There was no answer. Jim took advantage of the bright moonlight, though, to look around the room that was his prison.

He had been correct in his surmise. It was a cellar of some sort, but he didn't think this was the basement to a house. Instead, it was more like a root cellar or a storm cellar . . .

Then something was dropped into the cellar. Whatever it was, was sputtering and smoking, and giving off the very distinctive aroma of burning cordite.

Jim felt a quick surge of fear and energy when he realized that what had been tossed into this small, confined room with him was a stick of dynamite, with a burning fuse!

THE WILD WILD WEST™

ROBERT VAUGHAN

BERKLEY BOULEVARD BOOKS, NEW YORK

THE WILD WILD WEST

A Berkley Boulevard Book / published by arrangement with
Viacom Consumer Products, Inc.

PRINTING HISTORY
Berkley Boulevard edition / June 1998

The Penguin Putnam Inc. World Wide Web site address is
http://www.penguinputnam.com

ISBN: 0-425-16372-5

BERKLEY BOULEVARD
Berkley Boulevard Books are published by The Berkley Publishing Group,
a member of Penguin Putnam Inc.,
200 Madison Avenue, New York, New York 10016.
BERKLEY BOULEVARD and its logo are trademarks belonging to
Berkley Publishing Corporation.

PRINTED IN THE UNITED STATES OF AMERICA

10 9 8 7 6 5 4 3 2 1

THE WILD WILD WEST™

A small, three-car train raced through the night. In a private car attached to the end of the train, James West sat at an elegantly set dining table enjoying Tournedos Madeira. His dining companions were three beautiful young women: a blonde, a brunette, and a redhead.

The women had prevailed upon him for a ride from Lordsburg, New Mexico, to Casa Grande, Arizona, and Jim, in a spontaneous act of magnanimity, had responded. It was more than mere coincidence that the women were leaving Lordsburg at the same time as Jim. Their departure was sudden and unexpected, the result of the city marshal's raid on a theater where they were performing a show known as *History, Through the Art of Tableau Vivant.*

The show consisted of the three girls assuming studied poses to depict such events as Eve Being Tempted by the Serpent, Lady Godiva's Ride of Protest, and Renoir's

A Standing Bather. All were depictions of famous nudes, and although the ladies weren't actually nude when they posed, their close-fitting, flesh-colored body stockings on a dimly-lit stage made the audience think so.

The show played two times per night and filled the theater to capacity. The line outside the theater was three blocks long before every performance, and the show's popularity with the male citizens of Lordsburg between the ages of twelve and seventy caught the attention of the city's moral gatekeepers.

A committee of concerned citizens, composed of stern-faced women and sheepish men, called upon the three lady performers after the first week. Some of the men on the committee had themselves been patrons of the show and they begged, with their eyes, not to be exposed to the sharp-tongued shrewish wives who had dragged them to the confrontation. When the committee of concerned citizens failed to persuade the ladies to give up their performance, they filed a complaint of indecent exposure with the city marshal's office, resulting in the raid that closed the show.

''More wine, James?'' the redhead asked as she got up from the table and reached for the bottle.

''Thank you, Zelle, that's very sweet of you,'' Jim answered, holding his stemmed wineglass out.

''I'm Belle,'' the redhead said as she filled his glass.

Smiling, Jim looked across the table at the blonde. ''You're Zelle?''

''I'm Nell.''

''I'm Zelle,'' the brunette said.

''Then I propose a toast to Zelle, Nell, and Belle, three of the most beautiful—''

Suddenly the engineer applied the brakes for an emergency stop. Wine splashed from the goblet onto Jim's jacket. Belle, who had not yet regained her chair, was thrown to the floor, while Zelle and Nell hung on for dear life. Almost immediately, bullets came crashing through the windows.

"Someone is shooting at us! Down on the floor!" Jim shouted. Even as Jim was warning them, he was pulling a cord which caused steel shutters to drop down over all the windows. The firing continued, but now the bullets striking against the outside of the car had no more effect than if they had been hailstones.

Jim touched a button on the china closet, causing it to rotate one hundred eighty degrees and display an array of weapons on the reverse side. He took down a very peculiar-looking weapon which, upon close examination, appeared to be a miniature Gatling gun. He fitted a long magazine into the weapon, then he picked up something that resembled a billiard cue ball, and started toward the back of the car.

"What are you doing? Where are you going?" Nell asked.

"This will only take a minute," Jim replied, holding his hand out to calm them. "Please, enjoy a glass of wine."

"Enjoy a glass of wine? *Enjoy?* Are you crazy? Someone is shooting at us!" Zelle said.

"You're perfectly safe in here."

"He's right," Belle said. "Listen! The bullets are hitting the car but none of them are getting through." Belle looked at Jim with a puzzled expression on her face. "How can that be?"

3

"Nothing is too good for the comfort of my guests," Jim replied with a broad smile.

Jim carefully closed the door to the room before he opened the door that led out onto the back platform. As a result, he created a chamber of darkness so that no light would shine through to give away his position. In fact, with the windows closed, there was no light at all coming from the car.

In a dark patch of trees about fifty yards away, Jim could see the muzzle flashes of half a dozen gunmen banging away at the train. Grasping the little white ball firmly in his right hand, Jim jerked on a small wire lanyard which protruded from the top of the sphere. There was a popping sound, then a shower of sparks as the fuze began sputtering. With it activated, Jim threw it toward the gunmen.

The ball hit, then burst. It began burning fiercely, putting out as much brilliance as a flash of summer lightning, though in this case the luminance was sustained, like that of a distress rocket fired by a ship at sea. The effect was to render the area immediately around it as bright as day, and it exposed, quite clearly, the six men who were firing away at the train.

"What the . . . ? Where'd that light come from?" One of the attackers shouted. He was a tall man with a cadaverous face. He had no mustache, but he was wearing chin whiskers.

Jim put the butt of the Gatling against his hip. Taking hold of a special grip with his left hand, he began cranking the handle. The barrels rotated quickly, firing and ejecting shells as he turned the crank.

Bullets flew and popped into the night and the six men who stopped the train retreated into the darkness on the other side of the brightly shining bubble of light.

With the attack broken up, Jim hurried to the front of the train to see if any of the train crew had been injured. The engine was venting steam as if impatient to be under way. The engineer was in the window, which was backlighted by the glow of the firebox. Behind him could be seen the array of valves, pipes, levers, and dials of which he was the master.

"Anyone hurt up here, Mr. O'Leary?" Jim called up to the engineer.

"No one hurt, Mr. West," O'Leary answered.

"What caused the sudden stop?"

"Sure 'n would you be lookin' down the track, now, Mr. West, and tellin' me what you see?" O'Leary suggested.

Looking in the direction that the engineer indicated, Jim saw a fire in the middle of the track.

" 'Twas burnin' like the devil's own inferno it was, a few moments ago. I hope you'll be for pardonin' me for stoppin' like I did, but I could not take the chance of runnin' my train through it. Not without knowin' what was on the other side."

"You did the right thing, Mr. O'Leary."

At that moment a figure materialized out of the darkness between the engine and the fire. "Mr. O'Leary," he called. "No damage to the track. It's just some burning brush, is all. We can push right through it."

"Fine job, lad," O'Leary called back. Then to Jim, "Mr. West, if you'd be for returnin' to your car, I'll get us under way before those heathens who stopped us take a notion to return. We'll be in Sweetwater in less than two hours."

Jim waved, then returned to his private car. When he

stepped inside, the women were laughing and talking as if at a party, and indeed they were having a fine time, for they had taken his advice to enjoy the wine. One bottle was gone and they had started on a second, well on their way to being tipsy. They had also discovered Jim's "Edison Machine," and a cylinder-shaped recording was turning slowly as music poured from the tulip-shaped speaker.

"Ah! Our gallant hero has returned," Belle said, lifting her glass toward him. She sloshed some of the wine on herself. "Oops!" She laughed.

"Ladies, shall we return to our dinner?" Jim suggested.

"Dinner? Who cares about dinner?" Nell asked. "We're having a party!"

"Yeah, let's have a gay old time!" Zelle added.

Jim looked at the steak on his plate. No doubt it was cold now. Besides, he could always have the cook prepare Tournedos Madeira. And how often would he have the opportunity to enjoy three young women as beautiful as Belle, Zelle, and Nell? He smiled at them.

"All right, ladies, if it's a party you want, then it's a party we shall have."

He filled his own glass and lifted it to the bevy of beauties in his car.

When Emmet Tyson and the five men with him rode through the narrow pass in the Santa Estrella Mountains, their entry was noticed, and allowed by the pass guard.

Fifteen minutes after entering the mountain pass, the men exited into a valley. At the end of the pass and the head of the valley was a little town called Presidio. Architecturally, Presidio was like nearly most other towns in the Southwest, with adobe and unpainted lumber buildings gathered around a central square. Its location, however, in a valley that was protected on all sides by mountains and accessible only through a narrow, twisting pass, made it unique. With no railroad or stagecoach connections to the outside world, Presidio was completely self-contained.

The men rode directly to the stable, where they dismounted and began seeing to their horses.

"What's Cosgrove going to say about us showin' up empty-handed?" one of the riders asked as he removed his saddle and put it on a bench with other saddles.

"You let me handle Cosgrove," Tyson replied as he stroked his chin whiskers in contemplation.

"You want to deal with Cosgrove, you aren't goin' to get any guff from me," the first rider said. "I'd as soon stay out of his sight for a while."

Tyson turned his horse out into the pen, then started across the street to the Last Chance Saloon. He could hear piano music and loud laughter and conversation spilling out into the street.

Although Presidio had no book of statutes, and no town marshal or county sheriff to enforce them, that did not mean there were no laws. There were clearly recognized laws and rules of behavior, and anyone who violated those laws and rules could find themselves the recipient of a very vigorous enforcement from Presidio's self-appointed law enforcement officer, T. Marcus Cosgrove.

Cosgrove was the man Tyson was going to see, and he knew he would find him at the Last Chance Saloon, since Cosgrove normally held forth from a table there.

When Tyson stepped into the saloon, he saw Cosgrove just where he knew he would be.

Cosgrove had big shoulders, a barrel chest, and a bald head with a protruding brow. He was drinking a beer when Tyson came in, and he brushed the foam away from his mustache.

"How much did you get?" he asked in a deep, rumbling voice.

"We didn't get anything," Tyson replied.

Cosgrove set the mug down on the table and stared, hard, at Tyson.

"Are you trying to tell me that there was no money on that train?"

"No, I couldn't say that. We didn't even get a chance to look."

"Didn't you stop it?"

"We stopped it all right, but we couldn't get on board. It was a really short train, with only three cars. There was a fancy car hooked onto the tail end of it. That car was the one that caused us all the trouble."

Tyson went on to explain how the bullets couldn't penetrate the car, and how ten men, all armed, got off the train and started shooting at them. He could actually only swear that one man got off, but so rapid was the shooting that he was sure there were more men. Not even the fastest shot could operate a lever-action repeater as rapidly as the shots were coming.

"You ever see that car before?"

"No, nor nothin' like it, either."

"Damn," Cosgrove said. "Sure as a gun is iron, that car was filled with money. That's why they had it all protected like that."

"We should'a taken up a rail, instead of just settin' a fire on the track," Tyson said.

Cosgrove waved Tyson's suggestion off. "No, you did right. If we tear up the track, the trains will quit comin'. That would be like killin' the golden goose."

"But, what about that car?"

"Forget it. There will be other trains. And we'll still be here."

2

In Casa Grande, the train was shunted onto a side track. The three showgirls, who had decided to go on to California, were thanking Jim for the ride when the stationmaster approached. The stationmaster watched with envy as each of the beauties kissed Jim, then went into the depot to get the tickets they would need to continue their journey.

The stationmaster was a small man, with thin, brown hair that he tried to comb to cover the bald spot on top. He wore rimless glasses which, in the dark, reflected light from the gleaming lanterns that were hanging on the station platform.

"Would you be Mr. Jim West?" the stationmaster asked.

"I would be."

"My name is Pearson, Mr. West. I'm the stationmaster here." Pearson looked at Jim's private train. "I figured this had to be you. I was told it would be a rich fella with his own private train. Don't think I ever saw a private train before. I've seen a few private cars, but I've never seen a whole private train."

"Mr. Pearson, do you have something for me?" Jim asked.

"Oh, yes. There's a Russian fella waiting here to see you."

"A Russian?"

"Yes, sir. He says he's a prince, or a count, or something like that. Like as not you'll find him over at the Four Aces Saloon. That's where he's been hanging out for the last couple of days."

"Which one is the Four Aces?"

"You haven't been to Casa Grande before, have you, Mr. West?"

"Can't say that I have."

"I didn't think so. If you had, you'd know better than to ask which one is the Four Aces. Go out onto the main street. You can't miss it."

There were half a dozen saloons within walking distance of the depot, but the stationmaster was right when he said Jim would have no problem finding the Four Aces. It was the biggest, brightest, and loudest. The piano music, laughter, and conversation that spilled through its batwing doors was drowning out all other competition.

As Jim walked across the street, he could feel the ground giving back some of the day's heat. He heard a rider coming, the horse's hooves echoing hollowly in the night. He stopped, so as not to get run over. The horse materialized out of the darkness. The rider, a big man wearing a duster and a high-crowned hat, sat comfortably in the saddle, almost as if he were asleep. The horse and rider were visible for a moment only, then they disappeared back into the darkness.

Two men, far enough into their cups so as to make walking difficult, staggered out of the saloon, each of them holding a half-full bottle of whiskey. They were wearing the denim trousers and flannel shirts of working cowboys, and when they saw Jim in fawn-colored trousers, a dark blue jacket, and a ruffled shirt, they stared at him, their eyes swimming in their sockets as they tried hard to focus.

Jim knew what would be coming next. One of them would make some comment about the "fancy-dressed dude," and he would be faced with a choice of either responding to their insult and perhaps getting into an altercation, or walking away from them while they shouted epithets at him. Since neither option suited him, he decided the best thing to do would be to rush inside before their whiskey-sodden minds could react to him. He gave them each a slight nod of recognition, then he pushed quickly through the batwing doors.

As soon as he was inside, he stepped away from the door. He did that as a matter of routine, to deny an attractive target to anyone who might be hiding in the dark, watching him against the light of the saloon.

The Four Aces was considerably larger than the average saloon. Ten brilliantly shining chandeliers hung from the ceiling. The back bar, with a large mirror of fine-cut glass, added to the brightness by reflecting the light back into the room. The walls behind the bar, and all around the saloon, were covered with oil paintings of nudes in provocative poses. The bar was filled with patrons who hooked a boot onto the brass rail and leaned across their drinks protectively. A dozen or more painted women drifted through the room, working the patrons for drinks.

A sudden burst of laughter, followed by a groan of frustration, reached him from the far corner of the room. Looking in that direction, Jim saw several people crowded around a table. The center of everyone's attention was a medium-sized, dark-haired man dressed in a dazzling uniform of white, with gold trim. The uniform was resplendent with medals of all sizes, shapes, and colors. Jim had never seen an American uniform like this, so it had to be the Russian count that Pearson mentioned.

"Gentlemen, gentlemen," the Russian count said, raking in his winnings. "This game you Americans call poker, I must learn so I can take back to my own country."

"Count, you learn this here poker any better'n you know it now, and you won't be able to go back to your country. You'll be too weighted down with gold."

"Weighted down with gold!" the Russian repeated, laughing out loud. "I rather like that. Yes, I do like that idea, very much."

Jim walked up to the table. "Are you Count Sorenski?"

"At your service, sir. What can I do for you?" the count answered in a rather thick Russian accent.

"No, sir, the question is, what can I do for you? You asked to see me."

"My dear fellow. I am a Russian count, second cousin to His Excellency, the Czar, and a Colonel in the St. Petersburg Fusiliers. What could you possibly do for me?"

You tell 'im, Count,'' one of the men at the table said, and the others laughed.

"Well, Count, if you don't want to meet, that's fine with me," Jim said, turning to walk away from the table. "I never heard of you anyway before five minutes ago."

"You heard of me five minutes ago? In what capacity, sir?"

"That was when the stationmaster met my train and said you wanted to see me."

"Would you be Mr. West? Mr. James West?" the count asked.

"I am."

The count jumped up so quickly that his chair turned over behind him. He clicked his heels together and saluted, his hand quivering slightly over his right eyebrow.

"I beg your forgiveness one thousand times, and seven times more," he said. "I did not recognize you, Mr. West."

Jim chuckled. "No reason you should. I don't think we have ever met."

"Perhaps we could remedy that now," the count suggested. "I have a proposition for you. I am told that you have a rather remarkable train. I would like to hire your magnificent conveyance to take me on a sight-seeing tour of this marvelous Southwest territory."

Jim laughed. "Just like that, huh? You are going to invite yourself aboard my train?"

The count took an envelope from his pocket and handed it to Jim. "Would a personal request to you from the president of the United States make any difference?"

Jim took the letter from the envelope, read it, then put it back. He cleared his throat. "You have some powerful friends," he said.

"What about you, Mr. West? Are you going to be a friend?"

"We'll talk about it in my private car," Jim suggested.

"Splendid, splendid!" The count began taking his money from the table.

"Hey, Count, you ain't quittin' the table winners, are you?"

The count looked surprised. "My dear boy, have I misunderstood this American game of poker? I thought the object was to win."

Several laughed, and the one who had made the challenge looked down sheepishly.

"You gentlemen must learn to play without me, now," the count said. "I have business to discuss with this gentleman."

As Jim and the count started toward the door of the saloon, at least half of the painted women came over to tell him a very personal good-bye. He bantered with them all, calling them by name and offering his cheek to them for their kisses.

"You seem to have made quite a hit with the ladies," Jim said as they stepped outside.

"Yes, I do believe it is the uniform. Or, perhaps it is the medals. In fact, I'm sure that's what it is."

"And what, may I ask, do the medals represent?"

"You've got me, Jim." Suddenly the Russian accent was gone. "I picked them up at a costume shop in Denver. I chose only the biggest and the gaudiest."

Jim laughed. "Yes, well, never let it be said that Professor Artemis Gordon is understated. How are you doing, Artie?"

"Quite well, in fact," Artie answered with a chuckle. "I could enjoy being a Russian count."

"I'm sure you could, but I don't know if the Secret Service would continue to cooperate with you. By the way, that was a neat trick, showing me a letter from the president. But what if someone had seen that it was only an invitation to a party in New Orleans?"

"At least half a dozen people have already seen it."

"And they didn't blow your cover?"

"On the contrary, they have given the letter all the respectability it needs. I suppose it helped somewhat that none of them can read."

Both men laughed as they reached the railroad station, then stepped across the tracks and approached the car. Jim looked up to the top of the door, saw that the toothpick he had put there was still in place, indicating that the door had not been opened since he left.

"Still the cautious man, I see," Artie said.

"I try to be," Jim replied as he unlocked the door. Turning a switch just inside the door caused pilot lights to ignite the gas lamps, making the room bright. Artie went immediately, and knowingly, to the liquor cabinet. Reaching around back, he took out a bottle that was half-empty. The cork had been reseated with the palm of the hand, and Artie pulled it out with his teeth.

"My Napoleon brandy is still safe, I see."

"It's yours, Artie, and it will be here for you until you drink it up," Jim promised. "After what you paid for it, I wouldn't feel comfortable even sniffing the bouquet."

Artie poured the liquor into a snifter, then he held the glass out to examine it. The golden liquid caught the light from the gas lanterns, causing it to glow as if it had captured a bit of the fire. Artie passed the snifter under his nose, and inhaled the aroma. "Ah, Monsieur Bonaparte, what you missed by dying before you could enjoy this bottle." He took a measured drink, then replaced the cork, slapping it down securely with the palm of his hand.

"What's up, Artie? Why are we here?" Jim asked after giving Artie time for his ritual.

"You weren't told?"

Jim shook his head. "I received only a telegram, ordering me here. It said you would have all the information."

"And so I do. Or at least, I have as much information as there is available at the moment," Artie said. "Jim, have you ever heard of a man named T. Marcus Cosgrove?"

"Cosgrove? Yes, isn't he the one who tried to rob the army payroll at Fort Grant a few years ago? He was sentenced to fifteen years in Yuma prison, I believe."

"He escaped after serving only two years," Artie replied. "He's been out for over a year, and from what we have learned, it has been a busy year."

"What is he up to now?"

"Our old friend Cosgrove has served notice that he is seceding from the Union," Artie said. "He has declared himself president of a new country."

"And just where is this new country?"

Artie opened a cabinet and took out a book of maps. Turning through a few of the pages, he found what he was looking for.

"Here, in the Santa Estrella Mountains," he said. He pointed to a small town, surrounded by mountains. "It is sometimes called the 'Estrella ring' because the mountains completely encircle a small valley. At the head of that valley is the town of Presidio. As you can see, the only way in or out of Presidio is through *Paso de Morte*, the Pass of Death.''

"Presidio? Spanish for fortress. I can see why they would choose such a name," Jim said. "It truly is a fortress."

"And a fortress is exactly how Cosgrove uses the town," Artie said. "From Presidio he sends out raiding parties to rob banks, waylay stagecoaches, and hold up trains. Once they have the loot, they retreat back into their fortress."

"Why doesn't the army send a couple of troops of cavalry in to take care of it?"

"Because of the collateral damage the town would receive from a battle," Artie explained. "Presidio is actually a very old and established town, founded by the Spanish over one hundred years ago. Most of its inhabitants are innocent citizens, prisoners in their own town."

"What about Governor Morris and the Arizona Rangers? Couldn't they take care of the situation?"

"Governor Morris is afraid to do anything for fear it will endanger his daughter."

"His daughter?" Jim said.

"He has a twenty-three-year-old daughter named Amber. She was returning home from school when her train was stopped and robbed. When the bandits found out who she was, they took her prisoner." Artie pulled an envelope from his left front pocket and passed it over to Jim. "This is a picture of her."

Jim examined the photograph. It showed a girl with

large, expressive eyes and a fall of soft hair framing a very pretty face.

"She is a beautiful young woman," Jim said.

"Yes, and as I'm sure you can understand, the governor absolutely dotes on her. Our assignment, quite simply, is to put things right. We are to find Cosgrove, break up his gang, and bring him to justice."

"That's what I like about the people we work for, Artie, no ambiguity. A simple, straightforward order. Find Cosgrove, break up his gang, and bring him to justice."

"Yes," Artie agreed. "Though it would have been nice if they had suggested a way to do it."

3

Amber had been brought, on horseback, to the little town of Presidio. She wondered what was going to happen to her, and feared that she might be bound and gagged and thrown in some dark room somewhere. To her relief, she wasn't thrown in a dungeon, but was taken upstairs in what was obviously a hotel.

"This is where you'll stay," one of the men who captured her said, speaking in a low, gravelly voice.

"What? You mean here? This room is to be my jail?"

Her captor laughed. "We ain't got no jail in Presidio anymore. That was the first thing we closed up, after we took over."

After her captor left, Amber made a close examination of the room that she presumed was her prison. It was quite spacious and very nice, with a large, four-poster bed, a chest, a dresser, a small table with two chairs, and one larger, more comfortable chair which sat by the window.

Not only were her accommodations better than she expected; she also had plenty of clothes to wear. That was because when her captors took her from the train, they also took her luggage from the baggage car. In fact, when they put her in the room, they treated her as if she were a welcomed guest, and they actually asked her to tell them if she needed anything that would make her stay here more comfortable.

The only thing that would make her stay more comfortable, she thought, would be if she didn't have to stay here at all. She wanted to tell them that, but she knew they would only laugh at her, and she didn't want to give them the satisfaction.

For nearly an hour after her captors left, Amber did nothing but lie on her bed, frightened and confused by the mixed signals she had gotten. She offered prayers of thanks for not having been bound and gagged and thrown into a dungeon somewhere; yet at the same time prayed for deliverance.

Finally, she summoned up the will to get out of bed and walk over to the window. The window was actually a set of glass French doors that opened onto a balcony. The balcony looked out over the square of the little town and afforded a beautiful view of the mountains that surrounded the valley. She pushed open the doors, then stepped out onto the balcony.

As she stood there, she saw several people pass by on the street below her. Once or twice she thought about calling down to one of them, to tell them that she was a captive and to ask them please to notify the sheriff. The only reason she didn't was because she didn't want to put any of them into any danger. Also, she was certain that if she was heard shouting, her captors could reach her before any potential rescue.

Amber came to the realization then that she would not be able to depend upon anyone to come for her. If she was going to escape, she would have to do so on her own. That being the case, she returned to her room, then very quietly tried the door that opened onto the hallway.

To her surprise, the door wasn't locked!

With her heart pounding, both in excitement and fear, Amber eased the door open, then looked, very carefully, up and down the corridor. When she saw no one, she stepped out of her room.

With her back against the wall, she crept down the hall to the head of the stairs. Then, taking a deep breath and praying that she not be discovered, she went down the stairs. At the bottom of the stairs she looked around the corner of the wall and into the lobby. Thankfully, the lobby was empty except for the clerk. The clerk, whose back was turned, was busily writing at his desk.

This was where Amber had to make her first decision. Should she tell the clerk that she was being held as a prisoner in this very hotel?

Yes, she thought. Tell him now. She might not get another chance.

Amber started toward him, then changed her mind. Wait a minute! How could he not know? There was no way someone could be held captive in a hotel without the hotel clerk being aware of the situation. *He has to be one of them,* she thought.

Quickly, Amber stepped back behind the corner where she stood on the bottom step of the stairs for a long moment, trying to get up her nerve to cross the open lobby toward the front door.

Finally Amber took a deep breath, then walking quickly and staring straight ahead—as if somehow, by not staring at the clerk, he wouldn't be able to see her—she crossed the lobby.

Amber pushed open the front door and stepped outside, onto the sidewalk in front of the hotel.

She was free!

It was all she could do to keep from breaking into a run. She had to get away from this place. Obviously everyone in the hotel was involved in her imprisonment, or she wouldn't have been brought here.

Walking quickly, Amber started down the board sidewalk. She passed a general store, a saloon, a dry goods store, another saloon, an ammunition store, a leather store, and a shop that specialized in knives, until at last she was able to breathe easily. She was nearly two full blocks away from the hotel.

With her fear of immediate recapture behind her, Amber started looking around for the sheriff's office. She knew she had not passed one, but there had to be one somewhere. Where could it be?

A man passed by and Amber decided to take a chance.

"Excuse me, sir," she called to him. He stopped and looked back at her. "Could you tell me where the sheriff's office is?"

"The what? The sheriff's office?" the man replied. He began laughing out loud, as if what she had just said was the world's funniest joke. "The sheriff's office," the man said again. He slapped himself on the leg and walked away, still laughing.

Confused by the man's odd behavior, Amber pushed

24

open the door to go into the closest building. It was Spengler's Tobacco Shop, and the inside of the store was redolent with the rich smells of cured tobaccos. A man, whom she took to be Mr. Spengler, was sitting at a table, blending tobaccos. A woman, perhaps his wife, was standing behind a glass case. The glass case featured an array of pipes.

"Yes, Miss, what can I do for you?" the woman asked.

"I'm looking for the sheriff's office," Amber said.

Spengler turned toward her. "Presidio don't have a sheriff," he said. He got up from the table and walked over toward her.

"Surely it has something, a constable, a town marshal, some sort of law enforcement officer?" Amber said.

Spengler shook his head. "Only thing we got that comes close to someone like that would be Marcus Cosgrove."

"Who is Marcus Cosgrove?"

"He's . . . like the mayor," Spengler said, trying to explain Cosgrove's position.

"All right, Mr. Cosgrove, then. Where will I find him? I must talk to him."

"Honey, you don't want to go talk to that man," Mr. Spengler said gently. "He hangs out over at the Last Chance all the time, and the only kind of women who ever go in there are fallen women."

"I appreciate your concern, but you don't understand," Amber said. "I am a prisoner here. I was brought here against my wishes. I want to report it to this Mr. Cosgrove."

"My word, Miss Morris, do you think Cosgrove

doesn't know you are a prisoner here? He's the one who had you taken."

"What?" Amber asked, puzzled by the woman's strange response. "What did you say?"

"Sally said Cosgrove already knows you are a prisoner here," Spengler explained. "We *all* know you are a prisoner here."

"You . . . you all know?" Amber stuttered in disbelief.

"Tell her, Clem," Sally said softly.

"I think it would come easier from you," Clem said.

"Miss Morris, if it helps you any, we're nearly all prisoners," Sally said sweetly. "And we have been, ever since this was turned into an outlaw town."

Amber looked at Sally Spengler with a confused expression on her face. "I don't understand," she said.

"Some months back," Clem said, "Cosgrove and four or five of his men come riding into town. They started raising a ruckus and when the sheriff tried to put them in jail, they killed him."

"After that," Sally continued, "Cosgrove just sort of took over. There is no sheriff, and the jail has stood empty."

"Didn't anybody do anything?"

"What could anyone do?" Clem asked. "We are nothing here but merchants and clerks. None of us have any experience with this sort of thing. We figured if we would just mind our own business, he would go away. After all, what would a town like Presidio have to offer to the likes of Marcus Cosgrove?"

"Only he didn't go away," Sally continued. "Instead he brought more in, just like him. Now there are nearly as many outlaws in this town as there are decent folk."

"They rob and steal on the outside, then come back in here to be safe from the law," Clem explained. He snorted what might have been a laugh. "So here we are, in a town where the outlaws are free and the decent folk are prisoners."

"But I don't understand. What keeps the decent people in here? Why don't you all leave?"

Clem shook his head. "It's not as easy as all that," he said. "When you go back out into the street, have a look around. Have a good look around. This valley is completely surrounded by the Santa Estrella Mountains. There are no mountains in all of Arizona that are more formidable. Unless you are half mountain goat, the only way in or out is through *Paso de Morte.*"

"And Cosgrove keeps that well-guarded," Sally said. "Nobody gets in or out without his permission."

"Not even the U.S. mail," Clem said. "The stage-coach no longer comes in, the only freight in or out is what Cosgrove carries himself."

"Why won't he let you leave?"

Clem chuckled. "What good is it to own a town, if the town doesn't have stores or merchants? Cosgrove wants us to stay in business."

"Besides, even if we could leave, where would we go?" Sally asked. "We've got homes, businesses, and kids here. And I hate to admit it, but some of the local folks don't think it's so bad."

"Now, Sally," the man said.

"You know it's true, Clem. Nathan Algood, down at the Last Chance Saloon, has gotten rich since they turned this into an outlaw town."

"Well, who can blame him? You don't expect him to give his liquor away, do you?"

27

"No, but he needn't profit so much by it, either."

"We can't go calling the pot black when, truth to tell, we've done a pretty good business ourselves."

"Well, I thank you for your information," Amber said. "But I plan to have a few words with Mr. Cosgrove, whether it does any good or not."

When Amber stepped into the Last Chance Saloon a few moments later, her appearance so startled the customers that all conversation came to a halt.

There were four or five women already in the saloon, all wearing dresses so scandalously revealing that Amber wondered for a moment where a person could buy something like that. One of the girls walked over to her. The girl was young, and Amber decided she was probably pretty behind all the garish makeup.

"Miss Morris, you're free to go anywhere you want," the girl said gently. "But I don't think you want to come into here. This isn't a place for your kind."

"My kind? And what is my kind?" Amber asked.

"You know. Fine and decent," the girl answered genuinely. "Not like us." She looked down as if embarrassed to say so. "We're all soiled doves."

Despite her own situation, Amber actually felt sympathy for this young girl, and she wondered what would bring her to such circumstances.

"What is your name?" Amber asked.

"My name is Fancy," the girl replied. "Fancy Delight."

"Fancy, how do you know who I am?"

"Why, everyone in Presidio knows who you are, Miss Morris. We know you are the governor's daughter."

"And do you also know that I was brought to this

town against my will? That I am being held prisoner here?"

"Yes, ma'am. We know that too."

"This—this is outrageous. The entire town knows I am a prisoner here, and yet no one will do anything about it."

"No one *can* do anything about it, Miss Morris. Except Mr. Cosgrove."

"So I have been told. Fancy, I would like to speak with Marcus Cosgrove. Could you take me to him?"

"No need to take you anywhere," Fancy answered. "You're already here." She pointed toward a table at the rear of the room. "That's Mr. Cosgrove back there."

"Thank you."

Aware that every eye in the saloon was on her, Amber walked resolutely to the table at the rear to confront Marcus Cosgrove. Like the others, he had seen her come in and now, as she approached him, he stood and pulled a chair out for her.

"Hello, Miss Morris," he said. "Welcome to Presidio. Please, have a seat. Is there anything I can get for you? Wine, perhaps?"

"The only thing I want from you, Mr. Cosgrove, is my freedom," Amber said.

"Your freedom? Well, Miss Morris, you look perfectly free to me. Have you been restrained in any way? Tied to a chair, perhaps? Or locked in a room?"

"No."

"Oh, and by the way, all the merchants in town have been instructed to give you anything you want, without cost. Except for the gunsmith, that is. We feel it would be better for all concerned if we kept all weapons from you. I'm sure you can understand why. In the meantime, you are free to go anywhere in town that you wish.''

"I don't want to go anywhere in this town, Mr. Cosgrove. I want to go out of this town.''

"I'm afraid that is not possible, yet. Your presence here has created a rather delicate situation. We can't let you go until all negotiations are completed.''

"What negotiations?''

"Why, your father's government and my government, Miss Morris. Your father is the governor of Arizona Territory; I am the governor . . .'' Cosgrove paused, then laughed. "No, make that the king. Yes, that's it. I am the king of Presidio. King Cosgrove the First.''

"Oh,'' Amber said, putting her hand to her head. "The situation is hopeless. You are quite mad.''

4

In 1889 Phoenix became the fourth Arizona capital, after Tucson, Casa Grande, and Prescott. It did not yet have a permanent capitol building, so temporary offices were set up in the courthouse on First Street.

Jim and Artie were in those offices, or at least in the reception area of the governor's office. They were here to see Governor Morris, and according to the regulator clock on the wall, they had been waiting for nearly half an hour. Jim occupied his time during the wait by studying the layout of the office.

On the wall opposite the windows there was a calendar with a full-color Currier and Ives print of two night trains racing out of Washington, D.C.—sparks flying from the stacks, and every window in every car shining brightly. It was a dramatic, if unrealistic, representation. Just below the calendar was one of Edison's phonograph machines, and beside that, a small, potbellied stove. The stove was cool now as there was no need for it, but the faint aroma of smoke from last year's use still clung to the black iron. To the right of the stove was the door that led to Governor Morris's private office.

Every now and then Howard, the governor's "receiver," a bookish looking man in an ill-fitting brown suit, would glance over at them as if to determine whether or not they were still waiting. Finally, after sighing audibly to show these two interlopers that he had more important things to do than deal with them, Howard went into Governor Morris's private office. He stayed for a moment, then came back outside.

"Mr. West, Mr. Gordon, the governor will see you now."

"Thank you."

"And please don't take too much of his time. He is a very busy man," Howard called to them.

Governor Morris was a big man with mutton-chop whiskers and a bald head. When Jim and Artie came into the room, he looked up from some papers he was studying on his desk.

"Mr. West, Mr. Gordon, I'm sorry you had to wait so long. I'm afraid I have just been covered up in work today."

"We were prepared to wait for as long as it took," Jim replied.

"So it was beginning to appear," Morris said. "I apologize for my receiver. Mr. Parker's duty is to keep job-seekers and other petitioners away from me, but sometimes I'm afraid poor Howard gets a bit over-zealous."

"That's all right, General, no harm done. We are here now," Jim said.

Morris chuckled. "General. Not many people call me

that anymore. I must confess to liking it. Sometimes I wish I could go back to . . ." he stopped in mid-sentence, then sighed. "But . . . I'm sure you two gentlemen didn't come here to discuss my rather unspectacular military career. Now, what can I do for you?"

"General, we are here to investigate the rash of train-and-stage holdups and bank robberies that have been taking place in the Arizona Territory over the last few months," Artie answered.

Morris looked glum. "Yes, there have been a lot of them," he agreed. "You say you are here to investigate them?"

"Yes."

"Are you here under specific authority?"

"We are."

"May I inquire as to what authority?"

Jim took an envelope from his pocket and showed it to the governor. When Morris saw the return address, he blinked.

"The White House?"

"It is our letter of commission from the president of the United States," Jim said.

Governor Morris handed the letter back. "I am very impressed with your credentials, sir. You have my best wishes."

"Frankly, Governor, we thought that since Marcus Cosgrove was holding your daughter prisoner, your co-operation might be somewhat more active than mere best wishes," Artie said.

The governor's face grew pale. "You know about my daughter?"

"Yes."

"Please, Mr. West, Mr. Gordon, I beg of you, don't

33

say or do anything that would cause them to hurt her."

"Governor, we have no intention of doing anything that would harm your daughter. On the contrary, we plan to get her out of there," Jim said.

"No, you mustn't! Cosgrove made me swear that I would make no rescue attempts!"

"You won't be directly involved, General," Jim explained. "Artie and I will handle everything."

"But what can you do? There are only two of you."

"We can do more than you think."

Morris was quiet for a moment, then he sighed.

"If you would allow me, I am going to call in Mr. Gilbert Peabody. He is my attorney general and as such, is the chief law enforcement officer for the Arizona Territory."

"Go right ahead," Jim invited.

Governor Morris reached for the corner of his desk, where several wires seemed to congregate. Each wire was soldered to brass tack on a leather ring. In the middle of the leather ring, looking like the minute-hand of a clock, was a pivoting copper switch. Morris turned the switch to select a path, then pushed it down to complete the circuit.

A moment later Gilbert Peabody knocked once, then entered Governor Morris's office. "You rang for me, Governor?" He looked at Jim with obvious curiosity, but waited for the governor to speak first.

"Yes, thank you, Mr. Peabody. These gentlemen are James West and Artemis Gordon. They are agents with the Secret Service," Governor Morris said.

"Mr. West, Mr. Gordon," Peabody said, extending his hand.

"They want to try to rescue Amber."

Peabody looked at the Governor. "Sir, you remember that her captors were very emphatic in their warning to us, and quite specific as to what they would do to her if we attempted a rescue. I would strongly advise against it."

"Mr. Peabody, are you telling me, as chief law enforcement officer of the territory, that you would make no attempt to rescue Miss Morris?" Jim asked.

"I do this out of concern for the safety of the governor's daughter," Peabody said. "Cosgrove has threatened to kill her if we try anything."

"Of course he made the threat," Artie explained. "Cosgrove wants no trouble, so obviously he is going to do whatever he can to frighten you into inactivity."

"And you think that's all it is? A threat?"

"Don't get us wrong, Mr. Peabody. We do think, in fact we know, that Cosgrove is capable of hurting her," Jim replied. "Which is all the more reason we should attempt to get her out of there as quickly as we can. But for the moment I think she is far too valuable to them alive to be in any immediate danger."

"What, exactly, do you have in mind?" Governor Morris asked.

"Governor, really, I must caution you," Peabody said again. "Don't let these men push you into a precipitous action. If you do, I won't take the responsibility for what might happen."

"Seems to me, Peabody, as if that might be the problem now," Artie said. "You have taken no responsibility whatever."

"Are you accusing me of—" Peabody started in a stammering protest, but Governor Morris interrupted him in mid-sentence.

"Nobody is accusing you of anything, Gilbert. And don't worry, I will assume the responsibility for my own actions," the governor said. "I'm only ashamed I didn't take a more active role in securing my daughter's release before now. All right, Mr. West, what would you have me do?"

"I want you to make a money shipment. A large money shipment."

"How large?"

Jim smiled. "Well, since you won't actually be shipping any money, you can make it as large as you want it to be. One hundred thousand, two hundred thousand, even half a million dollars."

"I see," Morris said. "You're baiting a trap, aren't you?"

"Yes," Jim agreed.

"And the baiting of the trap, that is all the involvement you ask of me?"

"That is all."

"I would say that's enough," Peabody said. "Since your daughter is the real bait, here."

"Gilbert," Morris said. "My mind is made up. It's time to quit arguing and start cooperating."

"I'm sorry, Governor, of course you are right," Peabody said. He looked up at Jim and Artie. "All right, gentlemen, you will have our cooperation. How do you want us to make the announcement concerning the shipment of this money?"

"Why, I don't want you to make any announcement at all," Jim answered.

"Don't make an announcement? I don't understand. I thought the whole idea was to convince Cosgrove and his people that we were shipping a lot of money."

"Have you made any public announcements prior to any of the other money shipments?" Artie asked.

"No, quite the opposite," Peabody said. "We have attempted to keep the money shipments secret in order to prevent robberies."

"And have you been able to keep them secret?" Artie asked.

"I'm afraid not," Peabody admitted. "They have found out about them every time."

"Then don't you think a public announcement would make Cosgrove a little suspicious?" Jim asked.

"Yes, it might at that. Very clever, Mr. West," Peabody said. "Very clever indeed."

"If Cosgrove takes the bait, I'll be on board the train, waiting for him."

The southbound train from Prescott arrived just before three in the afternoon, and it sat on the track at the Washington Street station, popping and snapping as the heated gearboxes and connecting rods cooled. Because the trains were the town's principal connection with civilization, each arrival and departure caused a crowd to gather. As a result, the platform was filled with all sorts of people: townspeople and newly arrived passengers; miners in coveralls and great boots; farmers in homespun clothing; cowboys in jeans, chaps, and wide-brim hats; and children, laughing, shouting, and sometimes crying.

There was a new attraction today, as several people clustered around a buckboard, listening to an orator delivering a fiery speech. The bushy-haired, bearded, wild-eyed man was standing in the buckboard, jabbing his finger repeatedly at the crowd as he spoke.

"And here's another reason why there shouldn't be

no trains," he was saying. "It's been proved back east that them heavy trains shakes the ground so fierce that hogs is kept too nervous to eat. They don't fatten up none, and lots of folks is having to go without pig meat, which ever' one knows is a heap healthier for a body than just about any other kind of meat there is.

"Also, the live steam from the engines wilts the grass and spoils the pasture, and the horses and cows don't eat, and there goes your beef! And as if it warn't bad enough for the train to kill pigs, cows, and horses, why, it'll even kill little children what gets onto the tracks! And yes, old folks who are goin' to church in their buggy!"

He wagged his finger. "And hear this now! Them steel rails lyin' out there on the ground will draw lightning quicker'n a dog's tail, and ever' one knows to stay away from dogs during a lightning storm. Now, what do you think all that electricity runnin' around loose in the ground will do to you? It'll make you sturl, that's what.

"You know what sturl means, don't you? It means all the menfolk will be turned into geldings, and there won't be no more children being born. And if there ain't no more children, that'll be the end of the human race. I tell you, the world is doomed, unless you sign this here letter to the president of the United States tellin' him we don't want no more railroads, nowhere, nohow!"

"How many names you got on there now, Mister?" someone shouted from the audience.

"I don't have no names yet," the orator answered.

The crowd burst into laughter.

"But, I ain't a' givin' up hope," the orator insisted.

Again the crowd laughed, and Jim joined them. At that moment a bank courier, carrying a locked canvas bag and accompanied by two armed guards, arrived on the scene. The courier and the two guards looked around cautiously as they knocked on the door of the express car. This was the "money shipment" that Jim and Artie had arranged through the governor.

Though neither the courier nor either of the guards noticed him, Jim was watching their actions very carefully. If they were responsible for getting the message through to Cosgrove when a money shipment was carried, they might betray themselves in some way.

Jim also looked out over the crowd to see if anyone was showing more than passing interest in the transfer of the canvas bag. With so many people meeting each arriving and departing train, any one of them could be relaying information.

The door to the express car slid open and the agent inside bent down to take the bag. Because he wanted to ensure the integrity of the plan, Jim had not told the courier, the two armed guards, or the expressman that the currency notes inside were nothing but cut newspaper, and the coins, washers acquired from the local hardware store. They believed the shipment was real, and thus were behaving exactly as they would if it had been. That was important if the plan had any chance of working.

Not noticing anything out of the ordinary about the transfer, Jim maintained his position of observation long after the courier and guards were gone. As before, he watched the crowd. Not until the train had already started rolling out of the station did he run to catch up with it then hop on board.

Jim stood on the deck of the rear car as the train passed by the buckboard and the orator. He caught the gleam in the orator's eye and the two friends exchanged a short, almost imperceptible nod of greeting.

Artemis Gordon watched the train leave, having given no indication that he recognized Jim other than the very subtle nod. He had learned long ago that a person could sometimes disappear by becoming so obvious as to be overlooked. In his disguise as a somewhat mad orator delivering a ridiculous diatribe against the railroad, he had managed to provide a few moments of diversion to those who were gathered at the depot. And yet, though he had been the center of attention, not one person had seen beyond the buffoonish character he was portraying. By his very high visibility, he was able to mask his real purpose.

His speech was finished, and the crowd at the station had diminished considerably by the time Artie saw Howard Parker, the governor's receiver, go into the terminal building. Without being too obvious, Artie followed the little man inside.

Parker went directly to the Western Union window, where he wrote a message and handed it to the telegrapher. Artie moved over to the window as well, and stood directly behind Howard. Howard finished his message, then handed it through the window to the telegrapher.

"Same destination as the others, Mr. Parker? To Ristine?" the telegrapher asked.

"Yes," Howard replied.

The telegrapher looked up at Artie. "You want to send a message, Mister?"

"A message? A message? Yes," Artie said.

"Can you write?"

"Yes."

"All right, then, write it on the form, there," the telegrapher said. "I'll be with you in a minute."

Artie took one of the forms, then bent over it in thought as if composing a message.

As he left, Howard stared hard at the bushy-haired, wild-eyed man who was struggling with one of the message pads. He was absolutely certain he had never met the man, yet far back in the innermost chamber of his mind, there seemed to be a disturbing familiarity.

Artie made several illegible marks on the pad as he listened, and deciphered, the clicking and clacking telegraphy of the message Howard was sending.

MESSAGE TO J. K.

THE NEST IS EMPTY STOP WILL INFORM WHEN HEN SETS AGAIN STOP

PARKER

When the telegrapher finished transmitting Howard's message, he came over to get Artie's message.

"All right, let's have your message. Who is it going to?"

"It's going to George Washington, the president of the United States," Artie said, handing him the form.

"What?" the telegrapher replied, puzzled by Artie's strange statement. He looked at the form. "Here, what is this? This isn't writing! This is nothing but a bunch of chicken scratches."

Even though the train had already left, there were a few men still hanging around the station, and one of them, overhearing the telegrapher, laughed.

"Carl, you mean you wasn't out front a while ago listenin' to this fella carry on about the railroads? Why, you should'a heard him. Accordin' to him, the railroads is responsible for ever'thin' from drought to the plague. He's a crazy man!"

The others laughed out loud. The telegrapher, realizing then that he had been hoodwinked, grew flustered.

"Get him out of here," the telegrapher growled.

"No!" Artie shouted, pointing at the telegrapher. "I demand that you send my message to George Washington, the president of the United States! The railroad is evil, I tell you, and President Washington must be warned!"

"Come on, fella, I'll show you where George Washington lives," one of the men in the depot said in a condescending manner, and a couple of them led Artie, who was still fulminating about the railroad, outside.

The idea that this crazy man may have pirated the transmission of Howard's telegram did not occur to any of them.

5

Artie was just putting dinner on the table in the private car when Jim came in that evening, having taken the return train without incident.

"I thought you might be hungry," Artie said.

"Thanks, I am, and it smells very good."

"Have a nice trip?" Artie asked.

Jim shook his head. "Not a very productive one. I tell you, Artie, there is something to be said about traveling by private train," he replied. "This little misadventure took up a whole day. It was an hour to Maricopa, change trains, two hours to Tucson, then an hour wait before doing the same thing all over again, coming back. And all for nothing."

"Not entirely for nothing," Artie said as he poured a drink for Jim.

"What do you mean?"

43

"I did discover who is getting the information out, and where he is sending it."

Artie told Jim about seeing Parker come into the depot just after the train left.

"And you say he sent the message to Ristine?"

"Yes. I don't know the name, but it was sent to someone with the initials J. K."

"Ristine is very near *Paso de Morte,* the pass that leads into the Santa Estrella Mountains," Jim said.

"And Presidio, yes," Artie said. "I thought you might find that interesting."

"All right, suppose we see what we can find out about our mysterious J. K.," Jim suggested. He opened a filing cabinet marked from H to L, then pulled out a thick packet of cards.

"This will be our first chance to see if this crazy machine of yours works," Artie said, taking a sip of his wine as Jim made all the preparations.

At first glance, the cards in Jim's hand resembled playing cards. But upon closer inspection, it could be seen that, although approximately the same width as playing cards, they were almost twice as long. Also, the cards had a series of holes poked in them, in seemingly random positions.

Jim put the cards into a little box that had been constructed to the exact dimensions to hold them. Next, he connected the box to the top of a hand-crank-operated device that looked a little like the organ-grinder used by musicians who plied the panhandling trade with trained monkeys. On the same side of the machine as the crank there were two wheels, one wheel containing the twenty-six letters of the alphabet, the other, numbers from one to ninety-nine. Jim set the first wheel to J and the second wheel to the number eleven. Then, putting a lid down over the cards he had just put in the box, he began turning the handle rapidly. Most of the cards shot out from the back of the machine. There, they began stacking up into a receiving box. This box was built to the same dimensions as the feeding box.

Several of the cards, however, were kicked out to the side opposite the crank, where they fell into a third tray. When Jim finished running all the cards through, he picked up the cards that had been ejected to the side. Though not nearly as large as the stack he had started with, there was still a significant number of cards.

"These are all men with criminal records whose initials are J. K. They run from Jack Kabe to Justin Kyle. Now, let's run them through again to see how many are known to be in the Southwest territory."

Jim made a few adjustments to the machine, reset the letter and number wheels, then ran the cards through again. This time only twelve cards were kicked out to the side.

Jim picked up the twelve cards and reinserted them. Then he went back to the file cabinet, and after opening another drawer, came back with a single card.

"This is Cosgrove's card," he explained, holding it up. "I'll run it through the comparison slot. If there are any connections between Cosgrove and any of the twelve men we have isolated so far, then a hole in Cosgrove's card will match up with a hole in the card of the person we are looking for."

Jim fed Cosgrove's card into a single slot just below the feeder box, in which he put the twelve other cards. Then he turned the crank again. Most of the cards popped out at the opposite end of the machine, but two of them came out to the side. One of the two cards was that of Cosgrove. The other was one of the twelve. Jim looked at it.

"Did it come up with anything?" Artie asked.

"I think so," Jim answered, looking at the card. "This is the card of Joe Kitridge. It seems that Mr. Kitridge was in the Yuma prison at the same time as our friend T. Marcus Cosgrove."

"Last known address?" Artie asked.

"No known address," Jim answered. "But if I were a betting man, I would say you could find him in Ristine."

Ristine was built alongside the tracks of the Southern Pacific Railroad. Front Street, which was the most important street in the town, ran parallel to the rails. The Railroad Saloon sat directly across the street from the depot, and was Ristine's busiest watering hole.

Inside the Railroad Saloon a man sat at the end of the bar rubbing an ugly purple scar on his face and staring morosely into his drink. He had been in the saloon for over an hour, and this was his third drink. He was alone, despite the attempts by a couple of the bar girls to keep him company. He had even brushed off the bartender when he had tried to make friendly conversation.

One of the other patrons of the saloon, a gray-bearded man by the name of Pike, sat at his table near the cold stove, nursing his beer. Although the scar-faced man didn't know it, Pike had been studying him ever since he had come in. Finally Pike finished his beer, got up from his chair, picked up his hat, and started out of the saloon. As he passed by the scar-faced man he dropped his hat.

"Excuse me, Mister," Pike muttered. The scar-faced

man looked directly at Pike, glaring at him but saying nothing. Pike held his gaze for a moment, then recovered his hat and left the saloon. He walked a block and a half down the street from the saloon, then stepped into the sheriff's office.

Sheriff John Walt was just pouring himself a cup of coffee when Pike came in.

"Hello, Pike," the sheriff greeted. "Want a cup of coffee?"

"No thanks, Johnny," Pike replied, waving off the offer. "The one thing I don't miss about being sheriff is the coffee. You were a good deputy, but I swear you make the worst coffee in the world."

Walt chuckled. "Well, that was because I was just the deputy. Now that I'm sheriff, my coffee's pretty good. You ought to try it."

"Thanks anyway, but I'll pass," Pike said. He stepped over to a long table on the side of the room and began looking through a book of wanted posters.

"What is it, Pike?" Walt asked, coming over to the table. "What are you looking for?"

Pike scratched his chin. "I don't know exactly, maybe nothing. But there's a man over at the saloon that I don't think I've seen in Ristine before. He's got me curious."

"Is he wanted?"

"I don't recognize him as such," Pike said. "But I sheriffed for near forty years and this fella certainly has that look about him. Sort of a hangdog, always looking over his shoulder kind of a look."

Again, the sheriff laughed. "And that's how you would describe him on a wanted poster?"

"No. On a wanted poster I would say he is an ugly man with bushy eyebrows, a drooping mustache, and a puffy, purple scar that starts here, and comes down to here." He put his left finger to his face to demonstrate the size, shape, and location of the scar.

"Did he give his name?" the sheriff asked.

"No, he hasn't talked to a soul. Not even any of the girls," Pike answered. "That's another one of the things that makes me a little suspicious of him."

"I'll help you look through the posters," Walt said.

The old and new sheriffs stood side by side at the table studying the wanted posters, the room totally silent except for the measured ticking of the clock. After a few minutes, Pike sighed and closed the book with a solid thump.

"Well, I didn't see any paper on our mysterious stranger. I must be letting my imagination play tricks with me, thinking he was a wanted man. There was a time when that feeling was never wrong, but I guess I've lost my edge."

"John Pike lose his edge? Never," the sheriff said. "There may not be any paper on this galoot you described, but if you got a feelin' about him, then I'd be willin' to bet he's done somethin' somewhere." The sheriff walked over to the wall rack to get his hat. "You say he's over at the Railroad Saloon?"

"Yep."

"Maybe I'll walk over there and take a look at him myself. Which one is he?"

"Don't see how you can miss him, Johnny, he's the ugliest one in the place. You'll find him standin' at the south end of the bar, sort of starin' into his glass and not talking to anyone."

•   •   •

To the others in the saloon, it appeared as if the man with the scar was so lost in his own thoughts that he was oblivious to everything that was going on around him. But, in fact, he had already studied everyone in the room, and when the sheriff came in, he not only saw him in the mirror, but saw also that the sheriff was checking him over pretty closely.

Artemis Gordon ran his finger down the scar again. The glue was itching, but he dare not scratch it, for if he did the ''scar'' would crumble and disappear.

The sheriff stepped up to the bar beside Artie.

''What's your name, Mister?'' the sheriff asked.

Artie looked at the sheriff, but didn't answer.

''You heard me. I asked you your name. I'm not just making small talk here. I'm askin' as the sheriff of this town.''

''You got anything on me?'' Artie answered with a gruff voice. ''Any paper, any witnesses tellin' you I done somethin' wrong?''

''I'm going to ask you one more time. And if you don't answer me this time, I'm goin' to throw you in jail for interfering with an investigation. Now, what—is—your—name?'' He separated each word, making the question clear and distinct.

''Drago,'' Artie answered. ''The name is Drago.''

''Is that your first name or your last?''

''It's the only name I've got,'' Artie said.

''What brings you to Ristine?'' the sheriff asked.

''My horse brought me. What's it to you?''

''You're a funny man, Drago,'' the sheriff growled. ''Well, I run a quiet town, here. And if you do anything to disturb that quiet, I'll be down on you like a duck on a june bug.''

"Oh, I'm a quiet man, sheriff," Artie said. He lifted his glass and took in the saloon with a little wave. "You can ask anyone in here. I'm real quiet."

"That's the truth, Sheriff," the bartender said. "He ain't spoke more'n three or four words since he come in here."

The sheriff studied Artie a moment longer, then nodded. "Just see that you don't cause me no trouble," he said as he walked away.

Half an hour later, two men came into the saloon who caught Artie's attention. They didn't have the look of miners, cowboys, or farmers about them. And they obviously weren't men who worked in one of the business establishments in town.

One was big and clean-shaven. The other was smaller, with a thin, wispy mustache.

"Bartender, a drink for all the ladies," the larger man said cheerily, as he stepped up to the bar.

"No, make that two drinks for all the ladies," the smaller man added.

The women heard the invitations and, abandoning the men they were with, hurried over to the bar to join the two men.

For the next few minutes the two new men were surrounded by the women. They talked loud and laughed hard, and spilled liquor on the women and on each other. Their boisterous behavior and free spending quickly made them the center of attention of the entire saloon.

Not everyone found their antics amusing, however. In fact, one of the men whom one of the women was with didn't like it at all. When the woman abandoned him for her share of the largess being dished out at the bar, he protested. He reached out physically for her to keep her to him, but she twisted adroitly from his grasp and went over to join the others anyway.

The spurned man poured himself another drink, then another after that. Artie watched him in the mirror as he became more and more sullen. Finally, as if building up his courage, he took one last drink and got up from the table. He started toward the bar.

"Butrum, where you goin'?" one of the other men at his table called out.

"I aim to be gettin' Pearline back over here where she belongs," Butrum said.

"Why don't you just leave her alone? No sense in you goin' over there an' causin' any trouble. Them men's got money to spend. Let Pearline and the other girls get a little of it."

"Why don't you butt out of this?" Butrum slurred. "Ain't none of your business."

Butrum covered the distance between the table and the bar in a few determined steps.

"Hey, you! Kitridge!" Butrum called.

Artie's senses were alerted. One of these two men was Kitridge.

The bigger of the two men turned and looked coldly at Butrum.

"You got somethin' stuck in your craw, cowboy?" he asked.

"Pearline was with me. You got no right comin' in here an' takin' her away like you done."

"Oh, Butrum, don't get yourself in such a fix. Go back over there and sit down," Pearline said. "I'll be back with you in a little while."

"You better do what the lady says," Kitridge warned. "She's with me." He laughed. "In fact, they're all with me, now." He turned his attention away from Butrum, and back toward Pearline and the other women.

"There don't nobody take a woman away from me," Butrum said. "Leastwise, not and live to tell about it," he added.

Most of the people in the saloon thought Butrum's threatening words were the ravings of a drunken cowboy, and they were surprised when he pulled his pistol.

Artie alone wasn't surprised. He had been watching the scene closely and he had seen, in Butrum's eyes, the moment Butrum had made his decision to carry out his threat. In a lightning draw, Artie pulled his own pistol. Since he believed that Butrum really intended to shoot either Pearline or Kitridge, there was no time for him to issue a challenge. There was only time to act.

Artie thumbed the hammer back, then pulled the trigger. There was a sharp report as the primer cap burst; then the gunshot, sounding like a sudden clap of thunder. Artie's aim was perfect, and the bullet hit Butrum in the hand, taking off the end of his little finger and sending the gun flying.

Pearline and the other women screamed, and Kitridge and Spivey shouted in alarm when they realized how close they had come to being targets.

After that, there was a long beat of silence. The smoke drifted away and when it did, it revealed Artie standing away from the bar with a smoking gun in his hand, and Butrum holding his hand, trying to stop the bleeding.

"Did you see that?" someone asked.

"He had to be at least fifty feet away when he made that shot!" another added. "I ain't never seen anyone who could shoot like that."

"Butrum's bleeding to death. Somebody get a tourniquet on that man!'' the bartender ordered sharply. If it sounded at first as though the bartender was concerned for Butrum's life, his next remark showed his true worry. ''He's getting blood all over my floor.''

The sheriff, who had left the saloon after his brief interrogation of Artie, now came running back with his own gun in his hand. Seeing Artie standing there, still holding a smoking gun, the sheriff aimed at him.

''Drop it, Drago!'' the sheriff called.

''Sheriff, I—'' Artie started, but the sheriff pulled the hammer back and the ominous click of the sear on the cylinder could be heard all over the otherwise quiet saloon.

''I said drop it, or I'll shoot you where you stand!''

Artie dropped his gun. ''Now what?'' he asked.

''Now you're goin' to jail,'' the sheriff said. ''Which is exactly where I should'a taken you when I was here a few moments ago.''

''If you had done that, Sheriff, one of these men, and likely Pearline too, would be dead and you'd be taking Butrum in for a hanging,'' the bartender said.

''Yeah,'' said one of the men who had been sitting at the table with Butrum. ''That fella Drago shot the gun out of Butrum's hand.''

The sheriff looked incredulous. ''Are you that good with a gun, Drago?'' he asked.

''I'm as good as I need to be,'' Artie answered.

''Yeah?'' the sheriff replied. ''Well, for all I know, you could'a been tryin' to kill him, but you missed. Come with me.''

''Where are we going?''

''I think maybe you'd better spend a little time in jail.

53

Leastwise 'till I wire around to a few places and see if anyone is lookin' for you.''

Artie looked toward the two men whose lives he had just saved. Both of them avoided meeting his gaze. Instead, they turned away from him and, very pointedly, took a drink.

"Aren't you going to do anything, Kitridge?'' Pearline asked.

"Just what would you have me do?'' Kitridge growled.

Pearline pointed toward Artie. "That man, Drago, just saved your lives.''

"Yeah, well, we didn't ask him to butt in,'' the man with Kitridge replied. He and Kitridge went back to their drinking. They didn't even look around as the Sheriff led Artie from the saloon.

6

The streetlamp on the corner of First and Washington pushed enough light through the second-floor hall window of the courthouse to allow Jim to see where he was going. It was nearly midnight, and Jim was in the upstairs corridor of the building that was serving as the temporary capitol building.

When he reached the door under the sign that read, "Office of the Territorial Governor," he tried it and found that it was locked. Unperturbed, he lifted his right foot, twisted the heel of the boot, then removed a lock-picking tool. Using the device, it took but a moment to unlock the door. Quickly, he stepped inside, then closed the door behind him.

Jim pulled the shades, then lit a candle and went over to examine the phonograph. Raising the lid of the machine, he reached down inside and removed the grooved cylinder that was attached. Laying that one to one side, he replaced it with the one he had brought with him, a smooth, uncut wax cylinder. With the cylinder in place, Jim moved the recording needle into position, then wound up the spring so that when the on and off switch was moved, the turn-spool would begin operation. After that, he positioned the needle over the wax and turned the big, open-mouthed speaker horn slightly to the left, so that it was pointing more directly toward Parker's desk.

With that done, Jim attached a telegraph key to the underneath side of the machine in such a way that when the telegraph key moved, the on-switch would move with it. He ran a wire from the telegraph key so that it came out underneath the machine. He wrapped the wire around the leg so that it wouldn't hang down in obvious sight, then passed it behind the stove which sat next to the phonograph, then under the carpet, up behind the window curtain, to the window itself. Blowing out the candle, Jim raised the shade, opened the window, and crawled out onto the ledge. From there, with the coil of wire in his hand, he climbed out onto the roof, where he attached the wire to the lightning rod. He threw the coil across the arm of the pole that brought telegraph service into the courthouse.

Hurrying downstairs and outside, Jim retrieved the coil of wire, then started walking toward the railroad station, unwinding the wire behind him. On the other side of Washington Avenue he climbed another telegraph pole and looped the wire over the arm, thus elevating the wire as it crossed Washington so that it would be no different from the other wires that formed copper filigrees against the skyline of Phoenix.

From that pole, Jim ran the wire directly to his private

train car, which had been shunted off to a side track. Once inside the train car, Jim completed the job by connecting the wire to a battery and another telegraph switch.

Everything was ready now. Tomorrow, all Jim would have to do was wait, watch, and listen.

Jim and Artie had discussed whether or not Governor Morris should be told of his receiver's treachery. In the end they decided that Parker's involvement with Cosgrove would be information they would keep to themselves. It wasn't that they didn't trust the governor, but rather that they didn't trust the governor's judgment as to the people he selected to be around him. After all, if Parker was involved with Cosgrove, then some of the others on Governor Morris's staff might be as well. Also, as long as Parker did not suspect that he had been discovered, he would be less careful, and if closely observed, might reveal something helpful for the investigation.

The first thing Jim did, even before his nocturnal visit to the governor's office to plant his recording device, was to find the most expeditious place from which to observe Parker. To facilitate that, Jim had the engineer position his private railcar on a side track directly across Washington Avenue from the courthouse. The place he selected was perfectly aligned with the second-floor office where Parker worked.

With a telescope mounted on a tripod just inside the rear window of his car, the view of Parker's office was so unobstructed and the telescope so strong, that Jim could count the lit windows on the train cars of the Currier and Ives print on the calendar.

Sipping a nice claret, Jim spent the long morning observing the dozens of callers who visited the governor's offices. Some of the visitors were there to see the governor, while others remained in the outer office to conduct their business with Parker.

It was tiring to keep his eye to the telescope all the time, so sometimes Jim would have to take brief rest periods. Because of that, he almost missed the most significant visitor of the morning. He had just returned to the telescope when he noticed Parker's latest visitor. It was a tall man with a cadaverous face and dark chin whiskers. He didn't know the man by name, but he did recognize him. This was the same man who had led the outlaws in the attempted holdup of his private train a few days earlier.

He could see them clearly. But what were they saying? Jim reached over to operate the telegraph key.

With the movement of his finger a charge of electricity went from his telegraph key, up the wire from the train car, then from pole to pole across Washington, to the lightning rod on top of the courthouse, down the roof and in through Parker's window, behind the curtain, under the carpet, behind the stove and up around the leg, then through the bottom of the phonograph. There, the electromagnetic pulse initiated by Jim moved another telegraph key. This key operated the switch that released the tension on the turn-spool spring.

The cylinder started turning. As it did, the needle, vibrating to the sound waves that reached it through the speaker bell, started etching new grooves in the virgin wax.

"Tyson! What are you doing, coming here?" Howard asked, glancing nervously toward the door to the governor's office. "Don't you know that coming here is a very dangerous and foolish thing to do?"

"More dangerous for you than for me," Tyson replied.

"Why are you here?"

"Cosgrove wanted me to find out about that money shipment the other day. You sent a telegram saying there wasn't none, but we heard there was."

"You heard wrong. It was a ruse," Howard said.

"A what?"

"A trick. There wasn't any money. It was a plan to bring you out into the open."

"So, the governor has his courage back, does he? What did he do, call out the Arizona Rangers?"

"No, there are no Rangers. There are only two men involved, and they are from the Federal Government, not the territorial."

"Two U.S. Marshals?" Tyson laughed. "If the twenty-six Arizona Rangers can't defeat us, what makes anyone think two U.S. Marshals can?"

"They aren't U.S. Marshals."

"Well, if they ain't Marshals, what are they?"

"They are members of the Secret Service," Howard replied. "They have all the authority of the Federal Government behind them, and I am frightened of them."

Tyson laughed. "That don't mean nothin'. You're scared of your own shadow."

"No, I'm serious. There is something different about these two men."

"Yeah, well, you let us worry about them. You just find out when there's goin' to be some more money shipped."

"I'll do what I can."

"Do better'n that. I'll meet you this evenin' at the Palace Saloon. Have somethin' we can use, then."

Minutes later, Jim West showed up in Howard's office. His appearance so soon after Tyson left Howard unnerved, and he stammered as he greeted him.

"Mr. West," Howard said. "What . . . are you doing here?"

"Is there some reason I shouldn't be here?"

"What do you mean by that?" Howard asked nervously.

"I don't mean anything by it. Why are you so nervous?"

"I'm not nervous. I'm just busy, that's all. What do you want?"

"I would like to speak to the governor," Jim said. He glanced toward the Edison machine. The speaker horn was still as he had left it and, though it was hard to see, the wire was still wrapped around the leg of the phonograph.

"May I tell the governor what this is about?" Howard asked.

"No, I don't think so," Jim replied. "My business is with the governor, not with you."

Howard flinched, then he sighed, and stood up. "Very well, Mr. West. Wait here, please. I will see if the governor will receive you."

When Howard went into Governor Morris's private office, he closed the door behind him, just as Jim knew he would. That was what Jim was waiting for.

Quickly, Jim stepped over to the phonograph. Raising the lid, he removed the wax cylinder that he had installed last night. Then he lowered the lid and left the office. It was all over in a matter of seconds. He didn't really need to see the governor; it had merely been an excuse to get Howard out of the room.

"Mr. West, the governor will . . ." Howard stopped in mid-sentence, then looked around the room in some confusion. If West was all that intent upon seeing the governor, why did he not wait?

As soon as Jim returned to the car, he played the recording cylinder on his own machine. Although the recording was not as clear as it would have been had the two subjects spoken directly into the horn, he was able, by paying careful attention, to understand every word each of them said.

His experiment of capturing their words had been successful, both in validating his suspicion that Howard Parker was in league with Cosgrove, and in supplying him with Tyson's name. He also learned that they would be meeting, later, at the Palace Saloon.

In keeping with its proximity to the capitol building, the Palace Saloon was a large, brightly lit, and elegantly appointed saloon. It served a finer assortment of beer, wine, liquor, and liqueurs, and its clientele were better dressed and better behaved than that of the other saloons in town. Jim also noticed, as soon as he was inside, that the working girls were definitely better-looking. Their dresses, while more provocative than those worn on the street by ordinary women, were considerably more subtle and less revealing than the dresses worn by the bar girls in the other saloons.

Jim took a quick look around the room, but didn't see Tyson. He stepped up to the bar where, by looking in the mirror, he could make a more leisurely examination without being too obvious.

One of the more attractive of the girls came up to him. "Would you care for a little company?" she asked. "I don't want to intrude if you would rather be alone." Even the approach was more sophisticated.

Jim thought about telling her no, but he changed his mind. Having a woman companion would make him less obvious. He smiled at the girl.

"Well, I can't think of anyone I would rather spend a little time with," he said. "Please do join me."

The bartender, who had seen the whole thing out of the corner of his eye, put a glass in front of the girl and filled it without being asked.

"Thank you," the girl said. "My name is Michelle. What is yours?"

"My name is Jim. Michelle is a beautiful name."

"Thanks," Michelle said. She laughed. "That's why I chose it. It sounds much nicer than Mildred, don't you think?"

"Oh, I don't know," Jim said tactfully. "I think Mildred is a nice name, too."

"Do you want to stay here, at the bar? Or would you prefer a table?"

Jim weighed the options. From the bar, he had a better view of the room. But if Michelle had any information worth sharing, it would be better at a table.

"Let's take a table," he said, picking up both his glass and hers. They found a table near the back wall, and Jim put the glasses down, then held Michelle's chair out for her.

"Thank you," Michelle said.

"Have you been working here long, Michelle?" Jim asked when he sat down.

Again Michelle laughed. It was a pleasant laugh, like a gentle breeze whispering through wind-bells. "Are you asking me what a nice girl like me is doing in a place like this?"

"No, I mean how long have you worked here? How well do you know the clientele?"

The smile left Michelle's face and her mood changed. "It is no concern of yours, but I know them as well as I have to know them," she said coolly. "After all, I am a working girl."

Quickly, Jim reached across the table to take her hand in his. When he looked at her, his face was a picture of concern and contrition.

"Michelle, if you found the question insensitive, please forgive me. But I think you misunderstood. I am not passing any judgment here. I'm looking for someone and I understand that he sometimes visits this place. He is a tall man, with sunken cheeks and very dark chin whiskers. I don't know his first name, but his last name is Tyson."

Michelle shivered. "That would be Emmet Tyson," she said. "And I must say, I don't care much for your choice in friends."

"I didn't say he was my friend. I just said I was looking for him," Jim replied. "Do you know anything about him?"

"Why are you asking so many questions about him?"

"It's important, believe me," Jim said.

"I only know him when I see him. I've never even had a drink with him, though I do know that he always seems to have money, and is willing to spend it."

"Any particular reason why you've never had a drink with him? As you say, you are a working girl."

"He is a cruel man, who has behaved badly with some of the other girls," Michelle said. "I'm not the only one who won't have anything to do with him. None of the others will, now, even though he offers to pay two times, sometimes three times the money. Why are you looking for him, anyway? Are you the law?"

"Do I look like the law?"

Michelle examined him closely, then, as a small smile spread across her face, she shook her head. "If you are, you are the best-dressed sheriff or marshal I've ever seen. You know what I think? I think you are a gambling man, and Tyson owes you some money."

"Well, now, I can't put anything over on you, can I?"

7

Before Howard left his office that evening, he happened to notice that the speaker horn on the phonograph was slightly askew. He went over to adjust it and when he did so, saw that the turn-spool was empty. For a moment he thought someone had stolen the recording cylinder. His concern was eased, though, when he saw the wax roll lying loose at the back of the machine. Thinking it must have come loose, somehow, he reconnected it to the turn-spool and closed the lid.

"Howard, are you still out there?" Governor Morris called from his office.

"Yes, Governor, I'm still here," Howard replied. He hurried into Morris's office to see what the governor wanted.

"Did Mr. West ever come back?"

"No, sir, he never did."

"That's strange. I wonder what he wanted."

"I'm sure it was nothing important, Governor. He probably thought better of it, and that is why he left."

"It could be, I suppose," Morris agreed. "Howard, did you, by any chance, see a letter from Amber when you went through the mail?"

"I'm sorry, Governor, I went through all the mail. There was nothing from Miss Morris," Howard said.

The governor pinched the bridge of his nose and shook his head. "Why are they doing that?" he asked. "I have done everything those animals have asked of me. You would think they would at least have the decency to let her write to me," he said sadly.

Half an hour later Howard was thinking of the governor's lament as he walked through the alley toward the Palace Saloon. For a moment he had actually experienced sympathy for the governor, as well as a pang of remorse for what he had done.

As quickly as the remorse set in, though, it went away. All he had to do to get rid of the guilt was recall all the humiliation he had suffered at the hands of both the governor and his daughter.

For the entire time Amber was away at school, Howard had been a faithful correspondent. His letters had been breezy and informative, and she had answered him in a like fashion.

By the second year of writing to her, he was calling her by her first name. Amber responded by calling him her "dear friend," and she told him how much she looked forward to his letters, and how much she appreciated him for keeping her in touch with events back home. She also shared her observations of the school she was attending, and of the big city of St. Louis.

Howard lived for her letters. He believed himself to

be in love with Amber Morris, and he was certain that she reciprocated the feeling. But he was abruptly dis-abused of that illusion shortly before she was due to return home.

In one of her letters Amber had asked if Howard would mind meeting her at the depot. "What a glorious day that will be, for I shall have four years of accumu-lated longings for cherished and intimate sights," she said.

Howard was walking on clouds at the prospect. He was absolutely certain that the request for him to be at the depot when she arrived was her timorous way of telling him that she felt about him as he did about her. After all, didn't she mention how she was "longing for cherished and intimate sights"?

In his return letter, he was emboldened to tell her how much he loved her, and he asked her to marry him. He waited anxiously for her reply, and when it came, he read it as eagerly as a hungry man will devour his meal.

Dear Mr. Parker:

I have always welcomed your letters as if they were a visit from a friend, and I thought that was what we were. That is why I was not prepared for, nor did I welcome, your letter of the 4th, Instant.

Mr. Parker, if ever, in any of my letters, I said anything that would lead you to believe that there could ever be more than friendship between us, then I hasten to apologize. I assure you, sir, I have no romantic feelings for you, nor could I ever.

Under the circumstances, therefore, I feel it would be best if you did not meet me at the depot when I return. I believe we were, most certainly, viewing that encounter from different perspectives.

I have written my father with instructions not to send you to welcome me. I have also told him why.

Governor Morris had received his letter from Amber in the same posting, and he had called Howard into his office for a frank discussion.

What followed was even more humiliating. Howard could have accepted it much more easily if the governor had been angry with him. At least that would have meant that the governor was taking it seriously. It would have been a tacit admission that a romance between thirty-nine-year-old Howard Parker and twenty-three-year-old Amber Morris could be possible.

Instead, Governor Morris had laughed.

"What in the world got into you, Howard?" Governor Morris had asked amidst peals of whooping laughter. "Were you drunk? Did you really think, in your wildest imagination, that my daughter would say yes to you? Or that I would allow it, if for some strange reason, she did?"

"Governor, I realize the age difference is formidable," Howard had replied, "but—"

"Age? Why, man, don't you understand anything? Age has nothing to do with it. If you had been born on the same day you would not be a prospect for my daughter. I would hope that her sights are aimed higher than a file clerk. I know mine are."

It was shortly after that that Howard had conceived of the idea of having Cosgrove's men take Amber from the train during her return trip. It would not be hard to get the information through to Cosgrove. Howard was already working with the outlaw, providing him with information as to when money transfers were being made by the territorial government, or by a bank in Tucson, Casa Grande, or Phoenix. In return for his information, Cosgrove was paying him quite handsomely, and Howard Parker, ever the cautious and conservative man, had been putting the money away for a rainy day.

The irony was that he was now worth a great deal of money, more money than even Governor Morris had. Surely a man of such wealth would deserve a fair hearing with regard to marrying the governor's daughter. And yet he couldn't speak of it without exposing his criminal involvement.

When Howard told Cosgrove that Governor Morris's daughter would be on the next train, he suggested that she could be captured and held for ransom. What he did not tell Cosgrove was that he had some vague idea about rescuing her, with Cosgrove's cooperation, of course. That would make him a hero in the eyes of Amber and her father.

But Cosgrove had other ideas. It was his intention to keep the girl indefinitely.

"She's our protection," he said. "As long as we've got her, we won't have to worry about Morris sending the Arizona Rangers after us."

Howard wished that he had never told Cosgrove about Amber, but it was too late now. The fat was in the fire, and he would have to live with it. That being the case, he had no choice but to cooperate fully with Cosgrove, not only to make sure that he continued to draw his share of the money, but also to keep secret his role in the capture of Amber.

•   •   •

After a brief walk down what was called Melinda's Alley, Howard Parker reached the back side of the building in which the Palace Saloon was housed. He climbed a set of outside stairs that led to the second-floor entrance.

These stairs opened onto the Arizona Gentleman's Club, a private club that was located on the second floor. Membership in the Arizona Gentleman's Club was expensive and carefully controlled. In fact, it was so exclusive that few of the patrons of the saloon even knew of its existence. As a result, club members arrived and departed through the upstairs entrance with few of the saloon patrons even aware of their coming and going. That is why Jim, who was sitting at a table downstairs watching for Howard Parker to come in, completely missed his entrance when it happened.

Except for a table of diners sitting over in the corner, the Arizona Gentleman's Club was empty. They didn't acknowledge Howard as he walked through, nor did he speak to them. Howard had merely used the Club as an alternate entrance. He walked through the club, then out the door which opened onto the upstairs hall.

By arrangement, Tyson would be waiting for him in a room at the far end of the hall. The room was in the corner, with windows that looked out onto the street, the side of the building, and back into the alley. Because Tyson was a cautious man who was aware of the danger of ambush, he always chose this room.

Howard had just started toward the room when he happened to glance over the railing and down onto the saloon floor below. That was when he saw Jim West.

Howard gasped and backed quickly against the wall, far enough away from the rail to prevent anyone downstairs from seeing him. He stayed there for a long moment, pressing his back against the wall as if he could will himself to disappear. Then, cautiously, he slipped back up to the rail and took another look onto the floor below.

Yes, James West was still here. But what was he doing here?

West was sitting with a very pretty girl, but she certainly couldn't be the reason he was here. That girl was obviously a soiled dove. And though Howard had only recently met West, he would be willing to wager that Jim West did not consort with soiled doves. At least not professionally.

Then why was he here?

Suddenly a panicky feeling came over Howard. He was convinced that West was here looking for him. It was all he could do to keep from running. His breath was coming in ragged gasps. What should he do? What should he do?

Howard squeezed his hands into fists and tried to control his breathing with deep, measured breaths.

Wait a minute, he told himself. He began to get in touch with reason. How could James West possibly be after him? He hadn't done anything to arouse anyone's suspicion. West's being here had to be a coincidence.

Still, it was better to be safe than sorry. And the safest thing would be to find some way to get rid of West.

Forcing himself to be calm, Tyson made a mental list of the options before him. He could turn around right now, and leave before West even realized he was here.

No, that wouldn't work. Tyson was expecting to see him, and Tyson was not the kind of man one would break an appointment with. He certainly wouldn't want an angry Tyson to come looking for him.

Perhaps he should go downstairs and confront West, ask him straight out what he was doing here.

No, that wouldn't be good either. If West wasn't suspicious now, Howard's sudden and frightened confrontation would certainly make him suspicious.

He could tell Tyson about West. Yes! That was the answer to his problem. He would tell Tyson.

To Howard, Emmet Tyson was a frightening and dangerous man. Surely such a man could handle Mr. West. After all, James West wore fancy clothes and had expensive tastes. West had a private train and a gourmet chef to support his hedonistic lifestyle. West was nothing but a fancy-dressed dandy. And what chance would such a fancy-dressed dandy have against the likes of Emmet Tyson?

Having formulated a plan for dealing with the situation, Howard was able to pull himself together and hurry down to the end of the hall to keep his meeting.

Jim was frustrated and confused. He knew, from having listened to the recording, that Parker and Tyson had planned to meet in the Palace Saloon. So why didn't they show up?

During the course of the long evening, he avoided Michelle's subtle invitations to go upstairs with her. It wasn't that he didn't find her attractive. She was a very pretty girl. But there was no way he was going to leave with her and take a chance on missing Tyson or Parker.

Over a period of time, Michelle could make as much money from her share of the drinks, anyway, so she filled the time with the story of her life. As a result, Jim knew everything there was to know about her when he finally left the Palace just before midnight.

It had been an interesting conversation and an entertaining evening, but it had not been fruitful. Neither Parker nor Tyson had shown up.

As Jim started across First Street, a man suddenly stepped from behind the corner of the building.

"Get onto that buckboard." The words were low and menacing.

The man who had accosted Jim was carrying a yellow duster over his arm, and just beneath the duster Jim could see the large, twin muzzles of the end of a double-barrel shotgun.

"You're Tyson, aren't you?" Jim asked.

Tyson reacted in surprise. "How did you know my name?" he asked.

"I make it my business to know about people like you," Jim said.

Suddenly there was a flash of light in his head, then everything went black.

Howard knew just where to take Jim. He told Tyson about the old Grady homestead just outside of town. Last year Grady had given up trying to grow cotton, and went back to Mississippi. Since that time, either Indians or vandals had burned down his house, so that the only thing remaining was the root cellar Grady had built for the vegetables he had never grown.

"He hasn't come to yet," Howard said, looking at Jim. "Do you think he'll be all right?"

Tyson laughed. "What do we care whether or not he'll be all right?"

"It wasn't my intention to kill him. I just wanted to knock him out for a while."

"Yeah, well, sometimes when you hit people in the back of a head you knock 'em out, and sometimes you kill 'em," Tyson said. "It doesn't matter. We're goin' to have to kill him anyway," Tyson said.

"What? No! Why can't we just leave him here for a while?" Howard said. "I mean, he never actually saw me. I can get word to the rangers that he's out here, and by the time they come for him, you'll be gone."

"And what good will that do?" Tyson asked. "We'll be right back where we started. He'll just start looking again. Besides, he may not have seen you, but he did see me. And I don't know how he knew me, but he even called me by name. We don't have any choice. We're going to have to kill him."

"I . . . I don't want any part of that," Howard said, shaking his head.

"So you're telling me not to kill him?"

"No, I . . . I'm just saying, I don't want anything to do with it, that's all."

Tyson snorted what might have been a laugh. "You are really something, you know that? You didn't want anything to do with taking the girl off the train, but you wanted it done. You don't want anything to do with killing West, but you do want it done. The thing is, you just want other people to do the dirty work for you, while you keep your hands clean. Is that it?"

"You don't understand. It's just that I don't have that type of disposition, that's all."

"You mean you ain't got the grit," Tyson said. "All right, you go on back into town. I'll take care of it for you."

Howard, who had driven the buckboard out from town, now got into the seat and picked up the reins. He looked over at Tyson.

"How are you going to do it?" he asked.

Tyson reached down into his saddlebag, then pulled out a slender cylinder. He held it up so that Howard could see the stick of dynamite in the moonlight.

"Oh, my," Howard said.

"I think this will get the job done, don't you?"

"Yes," Howard replied "But don't do it yet. I would like to be well gone when it happens."

When Jim regained consciousness he was in a dark, dank place. From the musky smell, he surmised that it was a cellar somewhere, but he had no idea where the cellar was or how he had gotten to it.

When he moved, he became aware of the fact that he was in handcuffs and leg irons. He wanted to lift his cuffed hands to rub the bump on his head, but his movement was so restricted that he couldn't even do that. He tried to reach his boot to get to the lock-picking tool he kept in the heel, but he couldn't get to that, either.

Jim began looking around to see if he could orient himself, for even if he could get free of the restraints, could he get out of the cellar? Where was the door? Was the door locked, or barred from the outside? It was just too dark for him to tell. Then, quite unexpectedly, the door opened, and a silver splash of moonlight spilled down inside.

"Tyson?" Jim called. "Tyson, is that you?"

There was no answer. Jim took advantage of the bright moonlight, though, to look around the room that was his prison.

He had been correct in his surmise. It was a cellar of some sort, but he didn't think this was the basement to a house. Instead, it was more like a root cellar or a storm cellar.

"Hey!" Jim called again. "Tyson! Let me out of here!" He didn't really expect Tyson to let him out, but if there was someone nearby, he wanted his voice to be heard.

Something was dropped into the cellar. Whatever it was, was sputtering and smoking, and giving off the very distinctive aroma of burning cordite.

Jim felt a quick surge of fear and energy when he realized that what had been tossed into this small, confined room with him was a stick of dynamite, with a burning fuse!

8

It was nearly midnight and Artie was in Ristine, sitting on a bunk in the jail cell. He was playing solitaire by the ambient light of a lantern that hung from a stanchion just outside his cell door. The sheriff who had locked him up earlier this evening was gone for the night, but he had left a deputy in charge of the jail.

About an hour ago, someone had tossed a note through the window of Artie's cell: *Be ready. We will get you out at midnight.*

The deputy had made his rounds at about ten, but since that time he had done nothing but sit at his desk to read the newspaper and look through old wanted posters.

"Find something interesting to read, did you, deputy?" Artie called out to him.

"I know your mug is on one of these wanted posters," the deputy answered. "I'm going to find you, and when

I do, I'll get me some of that reward money."

"Shame on you, deputy. You are an officer of the law. You aren't eligible for reward money."

"You don't worry none about that. If there's a reward out for you, I'll figure out a way to get me some of it, never you mind."

"A clever man like you? Oh, I'm sure you will," Artie said. Artie looked toward the clock and saw that the minute hand was just about ready to click into position for the midnight hour. "Say, Deputy, do you suppose you could share some of your coffee?"

The deputy looked over at the pot on the stove, then back at Artie. Finally, he shrugged and stood up. "Might as well," he said. "It ain't comin' out of my pocket."

As the clock began chiming the midnight hour, the deputy took a cup over to Artie's cell and passed it between the bars. "Red seven on the black eight," he suggested, pointing to the cards spread out on the gray blanket of Artie's bunk.

"Thanks," Artie replied. Looking over the deputy's shoulder, Artie saw Kitridge and Spivey coming in through the front door. The deputy heard them as well, and turned.

"Somethin' I can do for you gents?"

"You just stay right there, Deputy! That's what you can do for us," a gruff voice ordered. "And get them hands up."

The deputy lifted his hands.

Spivey closed the door behind them and pulled down the shades. Kitridge motioned toward the deputy. "Drop your gun belt, real easy," he said.

The deputy unbuckled his belt, then let his gun slide to the floor.

"Now, open the cell door and let my friend out."

The deputy did as ordered, and Artie moved quickly to the gun cabinet to reclaim his gun belt. He strapped it on, then pulled the pistol and spun the cylinder, checking the charges in the chambers.

"What was it you said your name was? Drago?" Kitridge asked.

"Yeah, Drago," Artie answered.

"Well, Drago, did you think me an' my pard there was goin' to just forget what you done for us?"

"I didn't know whether you would remember me or not," Artie said.

"Well, you can put your mind to ease, 'cause there was no way we was goin' to forget. Not by a long shot. Not after you saved our lives by what you done in there."

"You boys ain't going to get away with this," the deputy complained. "The sheriff don't like it when folks breaks out of his jail. He'll get up a posse and come after you."

"Is that a fact?" Spivey asked. "Well, whatever he does, it won't matter none to you, 'cause you'll be dead." Spivey pointed his pistol at the deputy, and the deputy squinted his eyes in fear.

"No, don't shoot him," Artie said quickly.

Spivey lowered his pistol. "What do you mean, don't shoot him? He'll start yelling soon as we step outside."

"He's not going to yell, he's too scared," Artie said. "Look at him. He can barely stand."

"Well, I'm just goin' to make sure," Spivey said.

Artie pulled his own pistol and pointed it at Spivey. He cocked it. "I said don't shoot him," he repeated, this time in a cold, menacing voice.

"Hey, what are you doing?" Spivey asked in a frightened voice. "You're pointing that gun at me and I'm the one that's bustin' you out of here."

"Is anyone paying you to kill this man?" Artie asked.

Spivey looked confused by the question. "Is anyone payin' me to kill him? No."

"I don't kill anybody unless I get paid for it. And I don't let anyone around me do it either. What would happen if everyone just started killing people for free? The next thing you know, people wouldn't be needing my services, and I'd be out of a job."

Suddenly Spivey laughed. He lowered his gun, then put it back into his holster. "I don't reckon I ever thought about it like that," he said. "All right, I won't kill him."

The deputy opened his eyes, then seeing that he wasn't about to be killed, let out a long sigh of relief.

"Get in there," Artie ordered. With his pistol, he motioned the deputy into the cell, then closed the door behind him. Seeing that the deputy was no longer in danger, Artie started toward the front door. "I want to thank you men for getting me out of here. Maybe we'll run into each other again, some time."

"Hey, wait a minute! Where are you going?" Kitridge asked.

Artie looked at the two men suspiciously. "What do you mean, where am I goin'? What business is it to either of you?"

"None, I guess," Kitridge answered. "We just thought you might like to come to Presidio with us."

"Now why would I want to do that?"

Spivey smiled, broadly. "We're pards, ain't we?"

"Look, you broke me out of here and I'm grateful. I

told you that. But I'm not the kind that pals around. You men go your way, and I'll go mine.''

"You ever heard of a man named Cosgrove?" Spivey asked.

"Cosgrove?" Artie paused for a moment, as if trying to remember. "No, I can't say as I have. Who is he?"

"He's the man we work for," Kitridge said.

"And he's always looking for good men," Spivey added.

Artie shook his head. "No thanks, I'm not interested in punching cows."

Kitridge laughed. "He thinks we're cowboys," he said to Spivey.

"Believe me, Drago, you won't be punching no cows," Spivey said.

"It doesn't matter whether I'd be punchin' cows or not. I do better when I work for myself."

"You do better, huh? Tell me, Drago, how much money you got?" Kitridge asked.

"You two sure are a couple of nosey galoots," Artie said.

"Maybe," Kitridge answered. "But if I was to make a bet, I'd say you don't have two nickels to rub together. On the other hand, if you was to come with us, you might be able to do this." He smiled, and pulled out a roll of money and fanned it.

"How did you come by that?"

"We're always flush," Spivey said, producing his own roll.

"You would be, too, if you worked for Cosgrove," Kitridge promised.

Artie rubbed his scar, as if thinking. "Always, flush, huh?"

"Always," Spivey insisted.

Artie nodded. "All right. Maybe I'll give this Cosgrove fella a try."

Spivey was in front, Artie was in the middle, and Kitridge was bringing up the rear.

It was just after dawn. After breaking Artie out of jail, they had ridden for a couple of hours before making camp. Breaking camp just before dawn, they rode for another half hour and were now approaching the pass that would lead into the Santa Estrella mountain range.

"Stop here," Kitridge said from behind Artie.

Artie stopped, then twisted around in his saddle. "Why did we stop here? I thought we were going on into the . . ." Artie halted his question in mid-sentence when he saw that Kitridge was pointing a pistol at him.

"Hey, what is this?" Artie asked. He turned back around toward Spivey and saw that Spivey, too, had his pistol drawn. Artie was covered from both sides.

"Take your gun belt off and hand it over to me," Kitridge ordered.

"And do it slow," Spivey added.

"So, you fellas are my pards, huh?" Artie asked. "With friends like you two, I don't need any enemies."

"Don't feel bad about it; it's the rule," Kitridge said.

"What's the rule?"

"Whenever someone comes in here for the first time, they gotta be unarmed," Kitridge explained.

"It was the same with all of us," Spivey said.

" 'Course, you could just keep your gun now, and ride on," Kitridge said.

"But if you do that, you won't become one of us."

Artie sat for a moment, as if trying to decide whether

or not he wanted to do it. "All right," he said finally. "I'll give it a try."

Smiling, Kitridge held out his hand. Artie took off his gun belt and handed it to Kitridge, who then hooked it over the pommel of his saddle.

Artie kept his eyes open on the way in. He saw at least four guards who wanted to be seen and a couple who didn't want to be seen. He was pretty sure there may have been a few more that he didn't see. The pass was long and narrow, with steep walls on either side. At one point, the canyon had been filled in from either side, creating a choke-point so narrow that only one person could get through at a time. If a posse, or the rangers, or even the army tried to come in, they could be held up here by no more than three or four well-armed men.

At the other end of the pass there was a large, well-watered and grassy valley. And at the head of the valley nearest the pass was the town of Presidio.

"When do I get my gun back?" Artie asked.

"Soon as you meet the chief," Kitridge said.

As the three men rode through the plaza, they generated a lot of attention. Men and women came out of the stores and buildings to watch them pass, while children ran excitedly alongside. Artie examined the faces of those who were watching. Some were hard-looking, heavily-armed men, but many were citizens of the town who looked at him, talking urgently among themselves, as if trying to determine what effect the addition of one more gunman would have on their lives.

Artie felt an immediate sympathy for the men, women, and children of Presidio for being caught up in an adventure that wasn't of their own making. He couldn't show that sympathy, though, not even in his eyes, so he stared back at those who stared at him, and he did it with such evil intensity that most of the women and some of the men looked away in fright, unable to meet his gaze.

He actually recognized one or two of the outlaws from previous encounters with them. He wasn't worried about them recognizing him, though. For one thing, no two of them had ever seen him in the same disguise, and none of them had ever seen him as he really was. Also, Artie had long ago learned an elemental truth about disguises. One didn't merely assume the disguise of another person; one *became* another person. In that way you projected not only the outer trappings, but the inner persona of the one you purported to be.

Amber was upstairs in her room writing a letter to her father. This was the fifth letter she had written, but so far she had not heard anything from him. She knew her father wouldn't just neglect to write. Either her letters weren't getting out, or they weren't letting his come in. Or, perhaps, both.

She continued to write in spite of this, hoping that at some point her captors might relent and let one of the letters go through. In the meantime, whether the letters were being transmitted or not, she could feel a sense of connection to her father as she was writing them, and she was able to derive some comfort from that.

Through the open window, she heard the commotion generated by Artie's arrival and, curious, stepped out onto the balcony to see what was going on. She watched the three riders come onto the plaza from the south side. Two of them she had seen before, but the third was new to her.

The men crossed the plaza with half a dozen young

boys running alongside. They passed the well, then rode by just beneath her balcony. At that moment, the man in the middle, the one that Amber had not seen before, looked up at her.

He was a terribly evil-looking man, with an awful, disfiguring scar. Amber started to turn away from him, then a strange thing happened. She couldn't explain it, but it was as if his face suddenly softened for her. His eyes looked at her with such intensity that she was unsettled. It was as if, somehow, he had reached out to her with a message of support. But how? And why?

Amber turned away and retreated back into her room. She had been here too long. She wanted out of here so desperately that she was willing to believe she could see into the soul of one of Cosgrove's gunmen.

Artie knew that the young woman who stood on the balcony looking down at them was Amber Morris. He knew it because he had seen her photograph, but he was pretty sure he would have known it even if he had never seen her picture. He had read defeat and surrender in the faces of the townspeople who had come out to watch the arrival. But in the eyes of the girl on the balcony, he had seen only defiance.

"Wait out here for a moment," Kitridge ordered when they reached the front of the Last Chance Saloon.

"You don't know what you're asking, when you tell a thirsty man to wait in front of a saloon," Artie growled. "But I've come this far with your rules. I guess I can go a little farther. What about my gun? When do you return it?"

"When I come back," Kitridge replied, taking Artie's gun belt in with him.

Artie and Spivey sat on a bench in front of the saloon and waited while Kitridge went inside to talk to Cosgrove.

Cosgrove was eating. "Drago?" he asked, spooning chili-hot beans into a tortilla. "You say the fella calls himself Drago? Is he Mex? What kind of name is that?"

"I don't know," Kitridge answered. "He don't seem Mex, but I don't know what he is. All I know is, I never saw anyone could shoot like he can. Not even Barnes. He shot the gun right out of a man's hand from a good fifty feet away."

"That's pretty good shooting, all right," Cosgrove agreed.

"The man was goin' to shoot me in the back. Drago saved my life."

"You sure he wasn't just tryin' to kill the fella and hit him in the hand by accident?" Cosgrove took a bite from his bean burrito, and juice ran down his chin.

"I don't think so. I think he hits what he aims at. He'd be a real good man to have with us. That's why I brought him in."

"Yeah, well you should've come to see me before you brought him in. A lawman would give his eyeteeth to get in here. We've got to be very careful about that." He dabbed at the bean juice with a napkin.

"Believe me, Chief, this man is no lawman. He didn't even want to come in. Me 'n Spivey had to talk him into it."

"You talked him into it?"

"We busted him out of jail an' he was just goin' to go out on his own. He would have, too, if we hadn't talked to him."

"All right," Cosgrove finally agreed, finishing his burrito. "Bring him in." He licked his fingers.

Kitridge hurried to the front door and motioned to Artie. "Come on in," he said. "Cosgrove wants to see you."

Artie and Spivey followed Kitridge into the saloon. Kitridge and Spivey went directly to the table in the back where Cosgrove was just finishing his meal, but Artie headed straight for the bar.

"Hey, he's back here," Kitridge called.

"Beer," Artie said, ordering a drink and, apparently, paying no attention to Cosgrove.

The expression on the bartender's face showed surprise that someone who was being brought in for an audience with Cosgrove would show such disdain. For a moment he didn't move.

"I said beer," Artie said again, more resolutely this time.

"Uh, yes, sir, beer," the bartender repeated. Glancing nervously toward Cosgrove, the bartender grabbed a mug and filled it with beer.

"This here is the man I was tellin' you about," Kitridge said when he reached the table. "I apologize about him goin' over to the bar like that."

To the relief of everyone, Cosgrove chuckled. "It ain't your apology to make. Besides, looks like your man is thirsty."

"Drago, what are you doin'?" Kitridge asked nervously. "This here is Mr. Cosgrove."

Artie raised his mug as if toasting Cosgrove, but he didn't leave the bar. "Pleased to meet you, Cosgrove," he said.

"Kitridge here says you are a pretty good shot. Is that so?"

"Passable." With studied nonchalance, Artie took a drink of his beer. As he lowered the mug, it suddenly burst in his hand, the result of a bullet fired by Cosgrove.

Artie had to admit, it was an impressive show. He should have been more attentive, because Cosgrove had drawn and fired before Artie had the slightest hint as to what was about to happen. If Cosgrove had wanted to put that bullet through Artie's heart instead of his beer mug, he could have done so.

"How is that, Drago?" Cosgrove asked as he put his pistol away. "Is that passable?"

There was a shot glass on the table in front of Cosgrove. For his answer to Cosgrove's question, Artie drew and fired. The shot glass exploded into a shower of tiny shards of glass. Cosgrove, Kitridge, and Spivey only had time to shout in alarm and throw their hands up to protect their faces.

"What the . . . ? Where'd you get that gun?" Kitridge shouted in surprise as the smoke rolled away.

Artie smiled. "Now, Kitridge, you didn't really think I was going to let you completely disarm me, did you? I always keep a spare."

"Did you have that gun while you were in jail?" Spivey asked.

"As a matter of fact, I did."

"So you didn't need us to break you out."

Artie shook his head. "No, I didn't. But I did appreciate the gesture."

Cosgrove used his handkerchief to wipe the whiskey from his face.

"Very impressive, Mr. Drago. It's your call. What do you do now?"

Artie was still holding the pistol and he realized then that everyone was looking at him nervously. He smiled, then reached around to his back and stuck the pistol down into his belt. With the vest covering the pistol handle, it was easy to see how it had escaped detection.

"Kitridge and Spivey said something about my joining up with your outfit," Artie said. "If the offer is open, I'd be pleased to accept."

"You're crazy, Drago. You think Mr. Cosgrove would take you now, after all this?"

"The offer is still open," Cosgrove said. "Kitridge, give the man his gun."

9

As soon as Tyson tossed the stick of dynamite down into the root cellar, he slammed the door back over the entrance and slid the bar across to lock it. Then he ran to his horse, mounted it, and spurred the animal into a gallop.

Inside the cellar, the sputtering fuse provided a small degree of illumination, and while the light was welcome, it was also stark evidence of the gravity of the situation. Jim could see that the fuse was about twelve inches long. If it was burning at one-half inch per second, which he estimated it to be, then he had just over twenty seconds to do something.

Using the toe of his left boot, Jim pushed his right boot off. When the boot was off he squatted down and picked it up with his knees. After that, he worked the boot up between his legs until it was high enough for him to grab hold of the bootstrap with his mouth. Once he got the boot lifted with his mouth, he was able to use his hands, even though they were cuffed together in front of him.

Quickly, Jim twisted the heel open. Then, using the lock-picking tool, he opened the handcuffs, then freed his legs. Free now, he checked the stick of dynamite and saw that about ten seconds remained.

Jim picked up the stick of dynamite and started to pinch out the sputtering fuse. Then an idea came to him. Instead of pinching out the fuse, he moved over to the door. By the faint light of the fuse, he could see the door frame, and jumping up, he grabbed the door frame with his left hand, and hung suspended for a second. With his right hand, he pushed the stick of dynamite into a gap between the frame and the door. After that, he dropped back down to the floor and dived for the far corner, covering his head with his hands.

Tyson had ridden at least a hundred yards away from the cellar, and now he reined in and turned to look back toward it. He waited for what seemed to be a very long time.

He wondered if the fuse went out. If it did, he would have to go back and take care of it. That wasn't a prospect he welcomed. What if it hadn't gone out, but was just burning very slowly? If so, it could explode in his face as soon as he opened the cellar door.

Of course, there was also the possibility that somehow West could've gotten to it in time to snuff out the fuse. If so, Tyson wasn't going to play any more games with him. He would just shoot. . . .

Suddenly a bright flash of light filled the night. The light was followed a second later by a heavy, stomach-jarring boom. Tyson felt the pressure wave and he could see, against the starry sky, smoke and burning bits of residue. With a satisfied smile, he turned his horse and rode away.

Howard Parker woke the liveryman to turn in the buckboard and team. "You didn't have to wake me," the liveryman said. "You could'a just turned the team loose and come in tomorrow to settle."

"I didn't want to be charged for a full night," Howard said.

"I wouldn't of charged you for a full night, Mr. Parker. I trust you."

At that moment the sound of an explosion reached them. The liveryman jumped.

"Jumpin' Jehoshapht! What was that?" the liveryman asked.

"It sounded like an explosion of some sort," Howard answered.

"I'm goin' to climb up here and have a look around," the liveryman said, climbing the ladder to the hayloft. He looked all around.

"See anything?" Howard asked.

"Not a thing."

"Maybe it was just thunder."

"Could be, I guess. But if it was, it was the strangest soundin' thunder I've ever heard." He climbed back down. "The rig'll be costin' you a dollar."

Howard paid him, feeling a sense of relief that James West was no longer a problem, and that there was no way he could be connected to it. It was for that reason, more than squeamishness, that he had asked Tyson to delay doing anything until he was gone. And it was for that reason, too, that he had awakened the liveryman. If he had to now, he could prove that he was nowhere near the explosion when it occurred.

The concussion of the explosion had raised a lot of dust, and it was painful on the ears, but that was all. Most of the force of the blast had gone up and out. It had also blown away the door, so that when Jim looked around he could see a lighter patch in the darkness, and that patch was filled with stars. He was free.

At about nine o'clock the next morning Jim West, cleaned, rested, and showing no ill-effects from his ordeal, visited the offices of the governor of Arizona Territory. Howard Parker wasn't at his desk, but Jim heard his voice coming from the governor's office.

"Don't forget, Governor, you have an appointment at two o'clock this afternoon with an official from the Maricopa Water—"

"Good morning," Jim said, interrupting Howard in mid-sentence.

"Ah! It's you!" Howard shouted. He was so startled by Jim's sudden and unexpected appearance that he dropped the bundle of papers he was holding.

"Howard, what is wrong with you?" the governor asked.

"I . . . uh . . . was just startled, that's all," Howard stammered as he bent down to recover the papers that were now scattered all over the office.

"I'm sorry, I didn't mean to frighten you," Jim said easily. He bent down to help retrieve the papers. "Speaking of frightening, did either of you hear that explosion last night?"

"Explosion?" the governor asked. "No, I didn't hear any explosion. What time did it happen?"

"About midnight, I think," Jim said. "Wouldn't you say it was about midnight, Mr. Parker?"

"I . . . I really wouldn't know," Howard mumbled.

"But you did hear it, didn't you, Mr. Parker? Surely you heard it?"

"I . . . I have to go," Howard said. "I have work to do."

"I'm sure you do," Jim said, smiling at him.

Howard, sweating profusely now, gathered up the last of his dropped papers, then went over to his desk. Without asking for permission to do so, Jim went on in to the governor's office. He closed the door behind him, sealing Howard off from any conversation he would have with the governor.

"Mr. Parker's behavior was very odd, don't you think?" Morris asked. "I don't believe I've ever seen him acting like that. What was all this about an explosion?"

"It was a little adventure I got mixed up in last night. It's not important," Jim said.

"Whatever it was, it certainly made Howard nervous."

"Yes, I noticed that as well."

"What can I do for you, Mr. West?"

"I was wondering if you had heard anything from my friend, Mr. Gordon."

The governor looked surprised. "Mr. Gordon? No. Should I have?"

"Not necessarily. But sometimes when Artie gets in the middle of something, he has to find rather ingenious ways of communicating with me."

"Of course, if I hear anything from him, I will let you know," Morris replied. "I'll tell Howard to be particularly alert."

"It might be better if we left Parker out of it," Jim said.

Morris looked surprised. "Surely, Mr. West, you don't suspect Howard of any wrongdoing? Why, he has been with me for over five years."

"Tell me what you know about him," Jim urged. "Everything you can."

"I don't understand."

"What, exactly, do his duties entail? Where did he work before he started working for you? How did you hire him? Where was he born?"

Governor Morris laughed. "My, you are asking a lot of questions about him."

"They are important," Jim said.

"All right, I'll answer as many as I can. As I said, he began working for me five years ago."

For the next several minutes, Morris filled Jim in on everything he knew about Howard Parker and Gilbert Peabody. Jim took careful notes, thanked the governor for his help, then left. As he passed Howard's desk, he looked over at him.

"You know, Parker, I might have been wrong about the time of that explosion last night," he said. "I said it was just before midnight but as I think back on it now, it may have been just after. What do you think?"

"I . . . I'm sure I don't know," Howard mumbled.

"Yes, I'm sure you don't," Jim said with a smile that was nearly a smirk.

Howard was beside himself. West should be dead, but he obviously wasn't.

How had West escaped? Howard knew that he had been securely restrained in the root cellar. And he knew that Tyson had set off the dynamite charge, because he had heard it with his own ears.

How could West know about Howard's involvement? Howard had been very careful. He kept no books, he had no personal bank accounts, and he left no paper trail that would lead to him. Last night he kept himself out of sight at all times. He knew West didn't see him, and couldn't possibly have known he was there. And yet, today, West was almost tormenting him with his talk of the explosion.

When he returned to his railcar, Jim went right to work. From the file cabinet where he kept his information cards, he took two blank cards. These he put into a template, then began placing pins over the cards, aligning them in specific positions in accordance with information he had received from Morris.

Parker was from Arkansas. There was a matrix on the template card and, on that matrix, a place for Arkansas. Jim punched the pin through that very point in the card.

When Jim had punched holes through both of the cards, he put them into the feeder tray on top of the machine he called an Information Collator. Then, by setting the proper code with his alpha-numeric wheels, he was able to put all the cards through a process of comparison and elimination.

At the end of his operation he had matched Tyson, Kitridge, and Cosgrove with three points: criminal record, type of crimes committed, and current location. He also came up with another interesting match. Cosgrove's first run-in with the law had been at a military court-martial at Fort Riley, Kansas. Both Howard Parker and Gilbert Peabody had been at Fort Riley at the same time.

Jim had just finished with his information sorting when he heard a commotion. Looking through the window, he saw a railcar being moved out onto the side track next to his. This wasn't a private car, however. It was a railroad flatcar, loaded with several large crates. Curious, Jim went outside to investigate.

There were several men crawling around on the flatcar, untying ropes and disconnecting cables. Their work was being supervised by a short, thin man, wearing a dress shirt without a tie or collar, but rather with sleeve-garters; and a stovepipe hat. He was all over the car, here shouting instructions, there giving warnings, and in another place doing the work himself.

One of the cables had been cinched down very tightly, and when it was loosed it whipped around, slapping loudly against a crate.

"Here, my good man!" the man in the top hat shouted in alarm. "Please watch what you are doing! That is my gas envelope. I must trust my life to its proper function."

One of the first things to be off-loaded from the car was a painted sign. It was leaned against the front of the car, attached to stakes, the pointed ends of which showed dirt residue, indicating that it had been anchored many times in the past. Jim walked up to the front of the car to look at the sign.

DEATH-DEFYING

AEROSTATION

FIFTY CENTS TO WATCH

TWENTY DOLLARS TO MAKE AN ASCENT
PROFESSOR GARLAND P. THOMAS
AERONAUT

"Are you interested in aerostation, sir?" the man in the top hat asked.

"Aerostation?"

"The correct technical term for a balloon is aerostat. The ascension of same is known as aerostation. One should use the proper terms, don't you think?"

"Oh, indeed," Jim replied. "Are you Professor Thomas?"

"I am he."

Jim pointed to the sign. "Is it very difficult to do that? Make a balloon ascension, I mean."

"It requires great skill and physical dexterity, to say nothing of training and experience."

"And you have all this?"

"I can see where your questions are leading, sir. You are concerned about going aloft with me, because you don't know whether or not you can put your life in my hands."

Jim chuckled. "Something like that," he said.

"Well, my good man, you may put your fears to rest. I was trained in the art of ballooning by none other than the world famous Professor Thaddeus Lowe himself. You do know who Professor Lowe is, don't you?"

"He made ascensions for the Union Army during the war," Jim said.

"That is correct, sir."

"The war was a long time ago."

"Indeed it was, sir, but Professor Lowe is still very active in the field of aeronautics. He recently made a trip, by air, from New Orleans to New York."

Jim found that piece of information very intriguing. "You mean he actually flew somewhere? I thought balloons could only go up and down. I had no idea they could be navigated in controlled flight."

"There have been many fascinating advances made in the field of ballooning over the years," Thomas said. "For example, during the recent Franco-Prussian War, the French used balloons to overcome the siege of Paris. They flew mail and passengers safely in and out of the city while the Prussian army below could only look on in frustration."

"That's very interesting," Jim said.

"My boy, the time will come when balloons of great size will be built to carry passengers from city to city."

"What will they think of next?" Jim asked as he watched the workers off-load the various crates, boxes, and canvas bags that made up Professor Thomas's balloon.

10

The balloon and supporting apparatus were loaded onto three wagons, then transported to Phoenix Park. There, the process of assembling all the components necessary for making the upcoming ascension attracted a great deal of interest, and most of the townspeople gathered to observe. Jim was one of the most interested of the spectators as he watched Professor Thomas unpack the gas generator, envelope, and wicker basket, then lay out the various lines and hoses. A plan was beginning to form in the back of his mind, but in order to carry it out, he needed a more thorough understanding of the art of ballooning.

As Jim observed the preparations for launching a balloon, there was, in another part of the town, a young man who was conscientiously attending to his duty. Although Billy Bates was only fifteen years old, he more than held up his end of family responsibility.

Billy's father had been a railroad brakeman, killed two years earlier in a train accident. Now Billy had to help make a living for himself, his little sister, and his mother. His mother sold baked pies, but that brought in precious little. There wouldn't be enough money to enable the family to survive if Billy didn't work as a messenger for Western Union.

In addition to what he earned from Western Union, he was able, from time to time, to supplement his income by delivering non-telegram messages. He was sitting just outside the Western Union window, reading a copy of *Harper's Weekly,* when one of the court clerks summoned him with the information that the governor wanted a message delivered.

"Yes, sir!" Billy said, laying the magazine aside and putting on his delivery hat. He was pleased at the prospect, not only for the money he would earn, but also because he had never seen the inside of the governor's office, and he was looking forward to it.

He wondered if governors sat on something like thrones, like kings did. He bet that they did.

It wasn't a question he was going to get answered right away, however, because when he reached the courthouse, the governor was standing on the steps outside, waiting for him.

"Are you the messenger?" the governor asked.

"Yes, sir," Billy answered, disappointed that he wasn't going to get to see the inside of the governor's office.

"Do you know who Mr. West is? James West?"

"Yes, sir, I do know. He's the fancy-dressed fella that come ridin' into town on board that rich-man's train car

". . . the one that's a' sittin' down at the depot."

"That's him," the governor agreed. "I want you to put this message directly in his hands," the governor insisted. "Don't let anyone else see it."

"No, sir, I won't. Just Mr. West."

The governor gave Billy the message and a quarter. Since he normally got no more than five cents for such deliveries, he figured the message must be very important. There was another bonus to this particular task. He might not see the governor's office, but he was going to get to see the inside of that train car.

That promise didn't materialize, either. Billy knocked on the door of the car, and no one answered. He looked through the window, but saw only another door.

Maybe if he knocked on that door?

Billy tried to open the back door, but it was locked.

"Here, boy, what are you doing up there?" the stationmaster called. Then, recognizing him, the stationmaster's voice softened. "Oh, it's you, Billy. I thought it was some kid from town trying to break in."

Billy held up the envelope Governor Morris had given him. "Mr. Clark, I have a message from the governor for Mr. West," Billy said. "I was just trying to get his attention."

"He's not in there," Clark replied. "But you can leave the letter with me, if you want. I'll give it to him when he gets back."

"Thank you, sir, but I can't do that," Billy explained. "The governor wants me to put it in Mr. West's hands personally."

"Well, all right then, you might try lookin' for him down in Phoenix Park. That's where everyone else seems to be."

"Everyone else? What's going on at Phoenix Park?" Billy asked.

"You mean you don't know about the aeronaut whose come to town? He come in with the train this very mornin'. Unloaded all his stuff off the flatcar that's sittin' right there on the side track."

"I seen that car come in," Billy said. "But I wasn't payin' it no never-mind, and didn't have no idea what it was about," Billy said. "What'd you say it was?"

"Why, it's a balloon. And the fella that brought it in is puttin' the contraption together down at Phoenix Park right now. He's what they call an aeronaut. Like I told you, half the town is down there watchin' him."

"Thanks, Mr. Clark," Billy said, starting for the park at a run.

For a moment or two after Billy arrived at the park, he wished he could just be a kid. How much fun it would be to stand around here with the others and watch this balloon be assembled. And, wouldn't it be something grand actually to go up in one of the things, though?

Billy didn't have to ask someone to point out James West to him. He had seen him around his private car from time to time. So when he looked around the crowd, he was able to pick him out right away.

"Mr. West?"

"Yes?"

"This message is from Governor Morris."

"Thank you, son," Jim said, giving Billy another quarter.

Smiling happily over circumstances that combined to pay him ten times what such a delivery was normally worth, Billy put the quarter in his pocket, then forced himself to leave all the excitement and hurry back to his job.

Jim read the note from Governor Morris.

Mr. West:
    If it is convenient for you to do so, please come to my office as soon as you can. I have some information which I think you will find interesting.
                                           Morris

When Jim reached the governor's office a few minutes later, Howard was at his usual position in the reception room. This time he was considerably less startled than he had been before, but it was obvious that Jim's presence made the governor's receiver more than a little nervous.

"Mr. West, if you are here to see the governor, I'm afraid you will have to wait. He has someone with him right now. You should have made an appointment."

"I think he'll see me now. He sent for me."

Howard shook his head. "I know of no such summons. As I say, you'll have to wait."

At that moment Governor Morris stuck his head through the door that led into his own private inner office. Seeing Jim he smiled. "Ah, Mr. West, good, I thought I heard you out here. Come in, come in."

Howard looked at the governor in surprise. "You sent for him, sir?" he asked.

"I did."

"But how? You didn't say anything to me."

"I didn't want to bother you, Howard, so I used the lad who runs messages for Western Union," Governor Morris said.

"Very well, sir. I'll get a pencil and paper and be right in to take notes for you."

"That won't be necessary, thank you just the same," Morris said. He stepped through the door, then made a motion with his arm to invite Jim into his office. "Come right in, Mr. West."

Once inside, Governor Morris pointedly closed the door behind them. Standing by the governor's desk was a tall, thin man wearing denim trousers, a white shirt, and a sheriff's badge.

Seeing that Jim had noticed his visitor, Governor Morris wasted no time on formal introductions, but got right to the point.

"Mr. West, this is Sheriff John Walt, from Ristine," Morris said. "I believe he has a message for you, from Mr. Gordon."

"Good," Jim replied, as he and Sheriff Walt shook hands.

"I have to tell you, Mr. West, I'm not sure this is your man," Walt said. "The fella I'm talkin' about is about medium-sized, sort of rough-looking, with a scar here, and—"

Jim's laughter interrupted Sheriff Walt's description. "Sheriff, don't waste your time trying to describe Artemis Gordon. He is a man of a thousand disguises. You will never see him looking alike any two times in a row. Where is he, now? Is he all right?"

"Yes, I believe so. Assuming this is the right one. If so, he escaped from my jail," Sheriff Walt said.

"What makes you think that the prisoner who escaped is Professor Gordon?" Jim asked.

"Because when I was lookin' around in the cell, afterward, I found this little box. There was a note on the box sayin' I should come to Phoenix and give it to you. I didn't know how to find you, but I figured if you was for real, the governor would know about you. Turns out I was right.''

Walt handed a small box to Jim.

''I appreciate you doing this for us, Sheriff.''

''Well, I wouldn't of done it, iffen he hadn't left a badge in the box. The badge was real enough lookin' that it convinced me. Then, just to be sure, I read what he wrote to you. If you two really are workin' to stop Cosgrove and that gang of outlaws he's got runnin' with him, then you got my support. They've been a thorn in my side ever since I took over sheriffin' from John Pike.''

''John Pike?''

''He was sheriff for a long time before I was. I was his deputy,'' Walt said. ''Why do you ask about John? Have you ever heard of him?''

Jim shook his head. ''No, I can't say that I have,'' he answered. He nodded toward the door. ''Governor, does Parker know about this?'' he asked.

''No,'' Morris said. ''He only knows that the sheriff came to see me, but he doesn't know what it's about. I stopped him from coming in because of what you said the other day about keeping all this as quiet as we could.''

''Good. The fewer people we get invovled, the better our chances for success,'' Jim said as he opened the letter.

Jim

I found Kitridge in Ristine, just as we thought we might. As luck would have it, I was able to perform

107

*a small service for him and that service has landed
me in jail.*

*If there is such a thing as honor among thieves,
he will repay me, by attempting to break me out of
here.*

*My plan, Jim, if it works, is to be invited into
their stronghold at Presidio. If you receive this letter, then my plan has worked.*

So, what do we do next?

Artie

"If it's any help to you, Mr. West, my deputy overheard them talkin' before they left. Accordin' to him,
your man did go with them to meet Cosgrove."

"Good," Jim said.

"I'll tell you another reason I brought the letter to
you. Them other two, Kitridge and Spivey? They was
goin' to kill my deputy, but your man talked them out
of it. That makes him all right in my book, so if there's
anything I can do to help, I'd be glad to do it."

"Thank you, Sheriff, but you have already been a big
help," Jim said. "This letter is just what I was looking
for. I know now that my partner is inside Presidio. All
I have to do is figure out how to get in touch with him
so we can plan the next step."

Sheriff Walt nodded, then struck a match against the
iron side of the stove. "Communicatin' with him, now,
that's goin' to be a problem," he said as he held the
match flame under his cigar. "Unless you've got a
trained pigeon. 'Cause 'bout the only way a body is
goin' to get in there is fly."

• • •

The grates were open on the stove against which Sheriff Walt had struck his match. There was no need for them to be open—there was no fire, nor had there been for several weeks. However, the open grates had nothing to do with the temperature of the room. They were open because some time ago Howard Parker had learned that by leaving the grates open on the stove in the governor's office and opening the grates of his own stove, he could hear everything that was being said. The stoves and stovepipe worked like the speaking tube on board a steamboat.

On the other side of the wall, in the outer office, Howard Parker stood by the stove with a tablet and pencil in his hand, taking notes on what he was hearing.

"Mr. Gordon won't do anything to endanger my daughter, will he?" Howard heard the governor ask.

"I promise you, Governor, your daughter's safety will be one of Artie's top priorities."

"Mr. West, I'd best be gettin' down to the station in time for the next train to Ristine," the sheriff said. *"I'm glad I was able to be of some help, and don't forget, if you or the governor need me, you know how to get in touch with me."*

"Thank you very much for . . ."

Howard closed the grates before the governor could complete his sentence. Moving quickly, he managed to get back to his desk just before the door opened.

The governor walked with Jim West and Sheriff Walt to the door that led out into the hall. Shaking hands with each of them, he pledged the support of his office as he told them good-bye.

The governor closed the door behind them, then turned to Howard.

"Howard, I hope you aren't upset with the fact that you were kept out of that meeting."

"You're the governor," Howard replied. "I realize there are times when certain affairs should be kept quiet. I know how to keep to my place."

"It isn't like that, Howard. It isn't that I want you to keep in your place. It's just that Mr. West has made me take an oath of secrecy during all this, and as he is a lawman for the Federal Government, I must comply."

"I understand, Governor," Howard said.

"I hope you do, Howard. I value your friendship and wouldn't want to do anything to jeopardize it."

Howard waited until the governor returned to his office, then he pulled out a piece of paper and began writing. Somehow, he had to warn Cosgrove that he had a spy in his midst.

Under normal circumstances someone like Amber Morris, the daughter of the territorial governor, and Sally Spengler, the daughter of a German immigrant, would never have become personal friends—there was too much difference in their ages and social backgrounds. But these weren't normal circumstances, and Amber and Sally had become friends.

"My mother died when I was fourteen," Amber said, answering the question Sally had just asked. Amber had been shown how to blend the tobaccos; she was helping out primarily to have something to do that would occupy her mind and time.

"Oh, you poor child," Sally said.

"What about you, Sally? Do you have any children?"

Sally and Clem looked at each other for a long moment, and Amber could see the sadness in their eyes.

"I'm sorry," Amber said. "It was an indelicate question. Please forgive me."

"No, dear, it wasn't at all indelicate," Sally said. "Clem and I did have a child, a daughter. You remind me a lot of her, though she would be only sixteen now."

"Would be?"

"She died of the fevers, just over two years ago," Clem said.

Amber touched the older woman's hand. "I'm so sorry," she said.

"Such things happen out here," Sally said, squeezing Amber's hand affectionately. "It's a rough country."

"Sometimes I think it would have been better if we had stayed back in Missouri," Clem said.

"And work for slave wages for the Matthews? No, thank you, Clem Spengler. We made the decision to come out here together. And who is to say that what happened to Margaret wouldn't have happened in Missouri?"

Clem got up from his table and walked over to embrace his wife. It made Amber feel good to realize that, even under circumstances such as these, love could persevere for good people like Clem and Sally Spengler.

11

Artemis Gordon's many successes as an undercover investigator depended upon his abilities to assume the identity of whomever he portrayed. That required not only great skill in acting and disguise, but also an ability to project the persona others expected to see from such a character. As a result, the real Artemis Gordon was so buried beneath costume, makeup, and acting, that only those people whom Artie chose to let inside could ever see him.

Another talent that was absolutely vital, not only to success, but to survival, was Artie's ability to judge others accurately. He could put his life at risk by choosing to trust the wrong person, but there were times when that risk had to be taken. Artie believed that this was one of those times.

It was mid-afternoon and the Last Chance Saloon was nearly empty when Artie stepped inside. The piano was silent because the pianist was napping in a chair that was tipped back against the wall. Two of Cosgrove's men were involved in a quiet conversation at the other end of the bar with a couple of the bar girls. Three of the townspeople, men who were not affiliated with Cosgrove, were sitting at a table near the side wall, while Nathan Algood, owner of the saloon, was sitting alone at another table, going over his books.

The fact that Cosgrove was not in the saloon presented Artie with the opportunity he had been looking for. He wanted to have a private conversation with Fancy Delight, because he believed he had seen something in her demeanor that set her apart from the rest of the girls. He hoped she was here this afternoon so he could take advantage of the opportunity that was presented by Cosgrove's absense.

As luck would have it, Fancy was there, and she wasn't busy. When he motioned to her to join him at a table, she smiled prettily at him, then did so after collecting two drinks from the bartender.

Fancy put Artie's drink in front of him, then took a sip from her own glass as she sat down. Artie knew that her glass contained tea, and he knew that he would be charged as if it were whiskey. The difference in cost was how the bar girls made their money. Their value to the saloon was in the additional drinks they were able to sell to the customers.

"What is your real name?" Artie asked.

"Fancy Delight."

Artie picked up his drink and stared at her over the rim of the glass. "No, that isn't it," he said, quietly. "I'll be happy to call you that, Fancy, if that's what you want me to call you. But how is there ever going to be trust between us if you can't even tell me your real name?''

Fancy returned Artie's intense gaze, almost as if mesmerized by the soft depths of his eyes.

''What do you mean, trust between us?''

''Sometimes it is a very good thing to have someone you can trust, don't you think?'' Artie asked. ''Like, between us, for example.'' He made a motion with his fingers that included the two of them. ''But if there is to be that trust between us, then you must tell me your real name. Otherwise, we have nothing to talk about.''

''I talk with lots of men,'' Fancy said. ''I don't tell them my real name.''

''Oh? And what is it you talk about with these men? Is there any conversation that you can remember one minute after the person is gone?''

Fancy was quiet for a long moment, then, in a low voice she said, ''No. There is nothing I can remember, afterward.''

''It's because you have no trust,'' Artie said.

''My name is Hannah. Hannah Scruggs. And I don't know why I just told you that. That is something I have told no one, not even the other girls in here.''

Artie chuckled, softly. ''I told you why. You told me so you could win my trust.''

''On the other hand, why should I want to win your trust? As far as I'm concerned, the town would be better off if you would all go away. You, and all of Cosgrove's outlaws.''

''Do you really think I am just another one of Cosgrove's outlaws?'' Artie asked.

Fancy continued to stare deeply into Artie's eyes. ''I

don't know," she said finally. "I think you are different, somehow."

"I am different," Artie said.

"I don't know why I believe you, but I do."

"Fancy, I need your help."

"My help?" Fancy was confused by the request. "What could I possibly do to help someone like you?" she asked.

"Do you know Miss Morris?"

Fancy nodded. "She's the governor's daughter. Yes, I know her."

"I need to talk to her. Alone. Will you arrange it for me?"

"Honey, you don't need to be botherin' her none," Fancy said. "She's not our kind."

"What do you mean she's not our kind?"

"I told you, she's the governor's daughter. She's a quality lady. She went to some finishin' school back East, did you know that?"

"I have to talk to her, Fancy. It is very important."

At that moment the batwing doors at the front of the saloon were pushed open and a man came in. He was a little taller than Artie, and thirty pounds heavier. The thirty extra pounds wasn't fat. Artie knew that because he knew who the man was.

"Malcolm Kincaid," Artie said quietly.

"Who?" Fancy asked. Then when she saw him looking at the man who had just come in, she nodded. "No, honey that's a man named Barnes. Carl Barnes," Fancy said. "And believe me, he is a mean one."

"I don't care what he calls himself now, his real name is Malcolm Kincaid," Artie said. Artie had not taken his eyes off the man.

"Are you telling me that you and he had one of these moments of trust?" Fancy asked.

Artie smiled. "Yes, something like that," he said.

"Hey, you, piano player!" Kincaid shouted. "What are you doin' just sittin' back there. Start playin' the piano!"

The shout startled the piano player from his afternoon nap and he moved to the piano and began grinding out "Buffalo Gals" before he even looked around to see who had challenged him.

"Now, that's more like it," Kincaid said. Kincaid looked over at Artie and Fancy. The laughter froze on his face when he saw Artie, and he stared hard, as if trying to call up some long, repressed memory.

Finally, Kincaid pointed at Artie. "Hey! Don't I know you?"

Kincaid did know Artie, he just couldn't place him in this disguise. Five years ago Artie, then disguised as a snake-oil salesman, had made a case against Malcolm Kincaid. The case had been for murder, and Kincaid was tried, convicted, and sentenced to hang. Until this moment, Artie did not know that the sentence had not been carried out.

"What's your name?" Kincaid asked.

"Drago," Artie answered.

Kincaid looked at Artie for a long moment as if trying to call that name up.

"Drago? Is that a first name, a last name, or what?"

"It's a name," Artie said without elaboration.

"Yeah, well, I don't like the name Drago," Kincaid said.

"That's all right. I don't like the name Carl Barnes, either," Artie said. He paused for a minute, then he said,

"I like the name Malcolm Kincaid a lot better."

"What the . . . ?" Kincaid gasped. He pointed his finger at Artie. "Mister, who *are* you?" he asked again. He began scratching a three-day growth of beard.

"I told you who I am. I'm Drago."

"Well, I don't like you, Drago," Kincaid said. "I don't know why I don't like you, but I don't like you. So get out."

"And if I choose not to leave?"

"I didn't give you no choice," Kincaid said. "I told you to get out."

By now all conversation in the saloon had stopped. Even the piano was silent, ending in a few dangling and discordant bars of music. Everyone was riveted on the drama playing out in front of them: the bartender; the other two girls and the men with them; the three men playing cards at the back of the room; the piano player; and even Nathan Algood, who was so fascinated that he put down his pen and closed the ledger book.

Kincaid licked his lips nervously as he looked around the saloon. He realized now that he had become the center of attention. He had pushed it too far to back out.

"Don't do it, Kincaid," Artie said quietly.

"Don't do what?"

"Don't pull your gun on me. You'll lose, and you'll die."

Kincaid looked surprised at Artie's comment, then he laughed derisively. He had some justification for his confidence. He was quick, and had killed many men in face-to-face shoot-outs, though nearly all of them had been under conditions that gave him some advantage. On the other hand, this was just such a situation, for Kincaid was standing and Artie was sitting.

"Walk away from it, now," Artie said. "And I won't kill you."

"Mister, if you can sell that, you can sell snake oil," Kincaid said.

Suddenly, Kincaid made the connection between the man sitting at the table and the snake-oil salesmen who had played a part in his arrest five years earlier. Artie saw in Kincaid's eyes that he had been recognized.

"Snake oil!" Kincaid yelled, starting for his gun. "I know who you are!"

"Kincaid, no!" Artie shouted one last warning, but it was too late. Kincaid had already cleared leather and was bringing his gun to bear.

Then in a move that was as quick as thought, and executed so smoothly that nobody in the saloon saw how it was done, a pistol appeared in Artie's hand.

Kincaid saw the gun there, and the last conscious moment of his life was surprise. The two men fired simultaneously.

So quickly had events unfolded that Fancy was unable to get up from her chair. Instead, she could only recoil in fear and twist around as the bullet from Kincaid's pistol smashed through the glass of tea that sat in front of her, bored through the top of the table, and punched into the floor.

Fancy screamed, but her scream was masked by the heavy explosive pops of two guns being fired, one right on top of the other.

Kincaid's bullet missed, but Artie's found its mark. It plunged into Kincaid's chest, stopping his heart almost instantly. By reflexive action, Kincaid fired a second time, but by now his gun was pointing straight down, and this bullet went through the floor. He staggered back against the bar, then slid down slowly, winding up in a sitting position, already dead by the time he finished moving.

Artie flexed his arm while everyone's attention was riveted on Kincaid, and when he did so, the same spring action that had produced the gun from his shirtsleeve drew it back out of sight. By the time everyone looked back toward him, he was sitting calmly with his elbows on the table and his hands clasped. There was no gun in his hand. It was as if he hadn't even moved, and if the others had not seen the pistol in his hand when he had fired, they could almost believe that it had been someone else who had done the shooting.

No one had seen him draw and no one saw him put the gun away, but the fact that it had happened was undisputed, for Artie's adversary was sitting, dead, on the barroom floor.

For Cosgrove to occupy an entire town successfully and close off the only pass that led to the outside world, he needed help from a few trusted people on the outside. One of the most valuable of his outside people was in town now. He and Cosgrove were having a late lunch at the City Pig Café.

"Lambert, get out here. You got any pie?" Cosgrove asked.

Lambert, the short, chubby, red-faced owner of the restaurant, hurried out of the kitchen at Cosgrove's summons.

"Yes, sir, Mr. Cosgrove," Lambert answered obsequiously. "I've got apple pie."

Like the other innocent citizens of the town, Lambert

was dependent upon Cosgrove's good graces to continue to do business.

Cosgrove and Pike were just starting on their pie when Tyson and another man came up to the table. They stood silently for a moment until Cosgrove saw them.

"What is it?" Cosgrove asked, wiping his lips with the table napkin.

"It's about Carl Barnes," Tyson said.

"Ah, yes, Carl Barnes," Cosgrove said. He turned to his dinner partner. "Barnes is one of the men I was telling you about. I've never seen anyone better with a gun. And I've got five, maybe six more in here nearly as good. So, even if someone did sneak in here like you said, I'm not going to worry about it. Not as long as I've got men like Carl."

"Yes, sir, well, that's sort of the point of my bein' over here," Tyson said. "You ain't got him no more."

"Ain't got him? What do you mean? Did he leave?"

"In a manner of speakin', you might say he left," Tyson said. "He just got hisself killed."

"How? Where?"

"He was shot. Over at the saloon."

"Was it a fair fight? Or did somebody dry gulch him? Never mind, you don't have to answer that. I know it wasn't a fair fight. There's nobody in town that can take Barnes in a fair fight."

"Turns out there is someone who could take him in a fair fight, 'cause he just done it. It was slicker'n a whistle, they say."

"Did you see it?" Cosgrove asked.

"I didn't see it, personally. But Davidson, here, he seen it. That's why I brung him in to tell you what happened."

"All right, Davidson, what happened?"

Davidson was one of the two men who had been engaged in conversation with the bar girls. He was an outlaw with no particular skills, tolerated as a member of Cosgrove's gang just because he was a warm body when Cosgrove needed numbers. This was the first time he had ever been in a face-to-face conversation with Cosgrove, and he turned his hat in his hand nervously as he talked.

"Barnes just got beat, that's all. And he was standin' and the other fella was sittin' down when it happened."

Cosgrove looked at Barnes as if he had gone mad.

"That's impossible," Cosgrove snorted. "Maybe somebody was fast enough to beat Barnes fair and square if they were both standin' toe to toe. But nobody is so fast they could do it while they are sitting down. How did he do it?"

"Well sir, that's another part of it that's so strange," Davidson said.

"What do you mean, strange?"

"I didn't see the fella draw, and I didn't see him put the gun away. It was like one moment the gun was in his hand, and the next moment it was gone. You know what I mean?"

"No, Davidson," Cosgrove answered in frustration. "I don't know what you mean. Did the man have the drop on Barnes?"

"No sir. Barnes drew first—then somehow or other the gun was just sort of in Drago's hand, like I said— then he killed Barnes, then the gun wasn't in his hand no more. I don't know how to explain it no more'n that."

Cosgrove's dinner guest looked up from his plate in

quick interest. "Did you say the man's name was Drago?"

"Yes, he just joined up with us a few days ago," Cosgrove said. "Why, Pike, do you know Drago?"

The gray-bearded ex-sheriff nodded. "Drago's no outlaw, Cosgrove, he's the one I come here to tell you about. Accordin' to the letter I got from Howard Parker, Drago's real name is Artemis Gordon. I should'a figured that out when I searched every wanted poster we had and didn't come up with his name."

"Tyson, Davidson, get Kitridge and Spivey. They are the ones who brought him in here, and they're goin' to help you take care of the situation."

"Help us?" Davidson asked. He backed a couple of paces away from the table and held his hands up in front of him. "Hold on there, Mr. Cosgrove, I don't want no part of this. I'm a thief, I ain't no gunfighter. And I told you, I seen the way Drago handled Barnes."

"You don't have to call him out," Cosgrove said. "All you have to do is kill him."

"Kill him?" Tyson asked.

"Any way you can," Cosgrove said.

The Last Chance Saloon had begun filling up with curious townspeople even before the gun smoke had drifted away.

"What happened in here?"

"What was the shootin' about?"

"Lordee, lookit that!"

Barnes was still in the sitting position, leaning back against the bar. His head was tilted slightly to the left side. His left eye was drooped half-shut, and his right eye was open, but opaque in death. His lips were parted

123

and a little drool of spittle hung from his mouth. There was a dark, crimson hole over his heart. His right arm hung down to the floor, the hand palm up. The trigger finger of his right hand was still curled around inside the trigger guard of his pistol.

One of the first to come in had been Tyson. He spoke a few words to Davidson, then the two of them left.

Fancy watched them leave.

"Oh-oh," she said.

"What is it?" Artie asked.

"Tyson and Davidson left. I'm afraid they've gone to tell Cosgrove."

"Let them," Artie said. "It was a fair fight."

Fancy shook her head. "You don't understand Cosgrove. He's not like a real judge or a sheriff, or anything. He might do nothing, or he might decide to have you killed. It all depends on what mood he's in. You'd better go. Here, take this."

Fancy slipped a key into his hand.

"What is this?" Artie asked.

"It's a key to my crib. I live in a real small house down at the other end of the alley, behind the hardware store. Sneak out the back door now while no one is paying attention. Wait for me there."

"Fancy, I don't want to get you into trouble," Artie said.

"I won't be in any trouble. All I did was sit here," Fancy said. "Go on, before they get back."

Artie hesitated for a minute.

"Drago," she said, "this is one of those times you were talking about, isn't it? When you have to be able to trust someone?"

Artie smiled. "Yeah," he said. "I guess it is. Thanks, Fancy."

12

Nearly all of Phoenix had witnessed Professor Thomas's "aerostation," which he insisted on calling the balloon ascension. The problem for Thomas was that few had paid for the privilege.

"Why pay to watch it?" they asked each other. "Once the thing goes up, you'll be able to see it for free, from anywhere in town."

The naysayers were quite right, of course. It wasn't necessary to come to the park to see the balloon. Once it started going up, all anyone had to do was look up to see the great, black ball ascending majestically into the bright, blue sky.

Thomas reached an altitude of five thousand feet before he came back down. He returned to earth approximately five miles northeast of the city, but so accurately had he predicted where he would descend that the wagon was there, waiting for him when he came back down.

After bringing the balloon back and reinflating it, Thomas tried to provide rides for the adventurous. When he had no takers, he offered to tether the balloon for the timid.

"You don't understand, mister," one of the men in the crowd shouted. "Tetherin' it don't do no good. It ain't the goin' sideways that we're afeared of. It's the goin' up."

The others laughed.

"I assure you, there is very little danger involved when you are with an experienced aeronaut," Thomas said. "And I am one of the most experienced balloonists in the country."

"I'd like to go up with you," Billy Bates said.

Thomas smiled broadly. "Of course you can, son," he said. "All it will cost you is twenty dollars."

Billy thought about it. He had twenty dollars, and he wanted, more than anything in the world, to go up in the balloon. But the twenty dollars would put a lot of food on the table for his mother and sister.

"Twenty dollars?"

"Twenty dollars," Thomas said. "Little enough money to pay for an experience that you will remember for a lifetime."

"I . . . I don't know," Billy said. "Maybe I had better not."

Every fiber in Billy's body screamed to go. He had been fascinated with the idea of balloons from the moment he had first heard of them. To think that people possessed the means of flying like birds was the most exciting thing he could imagine. Only his extreme sense of obligation kept him from spending the twenty dollar gold piece to go aloft with Professor Thomas.

He stepped back into the crowd and hoped that someone else would decide to go up. He wasn't sure that Thomas would make another ascension unless he was paid to do so, and Billy so wanted to see the balloon go up again.

More than half of the town was gathered in Phoenix Park to see the spectacle, drawn by word of mouth and by advertising flyers. Prior to his first ascension, Professor Thomas had paid two young boys to deliver handbills he had printed to advertise the event.

Many of those present held the flyers in their hands, and some had even asked Professor Thomas to autograph the broadsides so they could keep them as souvenirs. But one of the men in the crowd found something that didn't seem right to him, and he caught Professor Thomas's attention.

"Hey, Thomas, it says in here that there will be a parachute leap from your balloon. When is that going to be? I'd pay to see that."

"I would, too," another said.

"Yeah, what about it, Professor? When are you going to do that parachute leap?"

"I'm afraid that is no longer a part of the program," Professor Thomas said.

"Why not? You've got it advertised here."

"Yeah, it says right here, 'Death-defying parachute leap.' Now, you advertise it; I want to see it."

"Yeah, me too," another added.

"I'm afraid that the young lady who used to make the parachute leaps for me left the show to get married."

"So, you're sayin' there ain't goin' to be no parachute leap?"

"I'm afraid not."

There were several groans of disappointment from the gathered crowd.

"You ought not to advertise somethin' that you ain't goin' to do," the first man complained.

"Yeah," another said. "To say you're goin' to do somethin', and then not to do it . . . that's fraud."

"Very well," Professor Thomas said. "I *will* have a parachute leap." He paused for a long moment, then smiled. "That is, if any of you gentlemen are brave enough to do it."

There was an immediate buzz of protest from the crowd, which began to dissemble, along with comments that Thomas was just trying to get out of what he had advertised.

"Come, come, gentlemen," Thomas said. "If any of you would care to make the parachute jump, I will give you a free ride in the balloon."

The bantering stopped, just as Thomas knew it would, and he smiled at them victoriously. "Well, now, how hard can it be? My last leaper was a woman. Are you telling me that a woman has more courage than any of you?"

When there were still no takers, Professor Thomas sweetened his offer. "I'll tell you what. If one of you brave men will jump, I'll not only give you a free balloon ascension, I will also pay you ten dollars."

"I'll do it," Billy said.

There was a gasp of surprise as everyone looked over at the young man.

"Billy, you don't want to do that," one of the men said. "You'll break your fool neck. Your mama and sister depend on you. What would they do if anything happened to you?"

"Will you pay the ten dollars now, before I go up?" Billy asked.

"No. Why should I do that? You haven't done anything yet," Thomas replied.

"I just want to make sure my mother gets it, in case anything happens to me," Billy said.

"Don't worry about your mama, Billy," one of the men in the crowd said. "If anything happens to you, I'll make sure she gets the money."

"We'll all make sure," another said.

"Thanks," Billy replied. He looked at Professor Thomas. "All right," he said. "I'm ready."

"First, I am going to pass around the hat," Professor Thomas said. "If I can collect a total of one hundred dollars from this crowd, I will take you up for the parachute leap. If I cannot collect that money, all bets are off."

There was another grumble of protest from the crowd.

"Come, come, gentlemen," Thomas said. "You challenged me on the fact that I was advertising a parachute leap. Well, here is your chance to see one. And it is the boy's chance to experience the greatest adventure of his life. Would you deny him that? Would you deny him the opportunity to earn ten dollars for his mama?"

"I'll pay my share," someone said, putting some money in the hat.

"I will, too," another said.

The hat went around the crowd, with several dropping coins and/or bills into it. Within a few minutes 108 dollars and 15 cents was raised. Thomas counted the money.

"All right, gentlemen, it looks as if you are going to see a parachute leap," he announced.

The crowd cheered.

"What do I have to do now?" Billy asked.

"Now, you don't have to do anything," the professor said. "At the appropriate time, all you have to do is step over the edge of the basket. I'll get everything set up for you."

Jim West was at the back edge of the crowd. At first he was going to protest that the boy was being subjected to danger in order to provide sport for the others. But as he looked into Billy's face he saw not fear, but excitement. Billy was a thrill-seeker. Jim knew about that. He was a thrill-seeker himself.

Fifteen minutes later, all was ready and the tethered balloon started its ascent. Billy was wearing a harness. Lines ran from the harness into the open end of a long stovepipe-looking cylinder. The canopy of the parachute was stuffed up into the pipe. According to Professor Thomas's explanation, when Billy leaped, it would pull the canopy out of the pipe. The canopy would then open like a large umbrella, and Billy would be gently lowered to the ground.

There was very little conversation among those on the ground as they watched the balloon go up. When it reached the end of the rope, it was approximately six hundred feet high.

One of the men in the crowd had a pair of binoculars, and he was watching the balloon through them.

"The boy is climbing over the edge of the basket now," he called to the others.

There was a collective gasp from the men and women in the crowd.

"There he goes!" the man with the binoculars shouted.

One of the women screamed as they all saw Billy's body start to plummet toward the ground. It fell only a short way, however, and then the parachute opened above. There was almost total silence as Billy floated down. He touched down about fifty yards away. He fell and rolled, then got up and waved at the crowd. There was an immediate reaction of cheers and applause. Billy Bates, one of their own, had made a parachute leap.

13

Artemis Gordon, now free of the makeup and clothing that had created the character of Drago, waited in Fancy's small house. After a couple of hours of waiting, he heard a light knock at the door.

He pulled his pistol, then moved to the window. Pulling the curtain aside, he saw that it was Fancy. He continued his inspection for a moment longer, looking up and down the alley to make certain that she was alone. Once he knew that no one was watching her, he opened the door.

Fancy stepped inside, then closed the door quickly behind her. When she looked around her house, the person she had known as Drago was gone. Instead, there was a stranger standing before her. Putting her hand to her mouth, she gasped in fear and took a quick step backward. "Who are you?" she asked.

"Fancy, don't be afraid!" Artie said.

"Where is Drago? What have you done with him?"

Artie shook his head. "Drago is no more. In fact, he never was." He turned his hands out as if introducing himself. "This is the real me, Fancy. My name is Artemis Gordon."

Fancy shook her head. "You . . . you can't be the same person. You don't look anything like Drago."

Artie chuckled. "I hope not. Drago was not a very handsome fellow."

Obviously still not convinced, Fancy put her hand on the doorknob, as if ready to bolt.

"Trust me, Hannah," Artie said softly. "I am who I say I am."

"Hannah? My God," Fancy said almost reverently. She put her fingers on Artie's face, as if trying to feel for herself the radical change in his appearance. "It *is* you."

"Yes."

Now that the shock of discovering a stranger in her house was over, Fancy suddenly recalled the immediate danger.

"Oh! I came to tell you! They are looking everywhere for you," she said. "Cosgrove has let it be known that he will pay five hundred dollars to anyone who kills you."

Artie smiled. "He must want to get rid of me pretty badly."

"Is it true what they are saying about you being a U.S. Marshal?"

"Something like that," Artie said. "I am a U.S. lawman, but I'm not actually a marshal."

"What are you doing in Presidio?" Fancy asked. Then she answered her own question. "Never mind, I know why you are here. You have come to get Amber Morris, haven't you? That's why you wanted me to take you to her.''

"I'm not here just for Amber," Artie said. "I have come to free the entire town from Cosgrove, and the rogues he has gathered around him."

Fancy let out a sigh of relief. "At last," she said. "We have all prayed for this day. When will the soldiers come?" Suddenly she put her hand to her mouth. "Oh, you must warn them. Cosgrove is making the pass even more difficult to use. He has two cannons, did you know that? And he has them aimed at the pass. When the soldiers try to come through, they will all be killed."

"There are no soldiers," Artie said. He thought it best, for the moment at least, not to tell even Fancy about Jim. It wasn't that he didn't trust her; but rather that she could not be forced to reveal what she didn't know.

"No soldiers? Who, then? More marshals? A posse?"

"No one else is coming, Fancy."

Fancy was both shocked and disheartened. "No one else is coming?"

Artie shook his head.

"But surely you don't expect to do it all by yourself?"

"I won't be by myself," Artie said. "You have already helped me, and I'm sure that there are others in town who will help me as well."

"You have more confidence in the people of this town than I do," Fancy said. "But if you insist upon recruiting help from the townspeople, be very careful who you ask. With a reward of five hundred dollars, there will be some, even among the citizens of town, who would betray you."

"I will be careful," Artie said. "And you must be careful as well. So the first thing I am going to have to do is find another place to hide. I can't stay in your house any longer. It puts you in danger."

"Where will you hide?"

"I'll hide in plain sight," Artie said.

Fancy looked confused. "I don't understand."

"It's just as well that you don't understand," he said. "Fancy, I still must see Miss Morris. Do you think you could get word to her?"

"All right, I'll take a message to her. But where could you meet? They will be looking for you everywhere. And if they think you have come for her, they will be watching her room."

"Tell her to come to the City Pig for dinner at seven o'clock," Artie said.

"Come to the City Pig? Are you crazy? That's almost as public a place as the saloon."

"Just get the message to her if you can," Artie said.

"All right," Fancy replied. She started toward the door, but Artie held up his hand to stop her, then stepped back to the window.

"Wait until I check," he said. Cautiously, he pulled the curtains aside and took another look up and down the alley. When he saw no one, he looked over at Fancy and nodded.

"It's clear," he said. "Go ahead."

Fancy nodded at him, then opened the door. Just before she stepped outside, she looked back toward him to tell him good-bye.

"What the . . . ?" she gasped in shock.

Artemis Gordon was gone!

For a moment Fancy was frightened and confused, and

she almost closed the door again to take a look around her house. But then she thought better of it. She didn't know how he had disappeared so quickly, but it was obviously intentional. Looking for him now would only increase the chances of his exposure. And hers.

A hornet's nest. That was the thing that came to Fancy's mind as she hurried through the town looking for Amber Morris so she could deliver the message.

Like hornets buzzing around their nests after someone had hit them with sticks, men, armed not just with pistols in their holsters but with guns in their hands, were buzzing about in highly agitated states. They were traveling in twos and threes and were leaving no stone unturned in what was obviously a search. She saw men looking under porches, and under, behind, and down inside watering troughs. They were even forcing the townspeople out of their homes and into the streets so they could go into private houses and search. There, with no regard for personal privacy, they overturned furniture, tore down drapery, and looked under beds and behind doors.

The intensity and desperation of their search would be funny if it weren't also frightening.

Fancy started toward the hotel, but the lobby was crawling with armed searchers. Not wanting any closer contact with Cosgrove or any of his men than was absolutely necessary, she decided to visit the tobacco shop. She knew that Amber and the Spenglers had become great friends, and there was always the possibility that she might find the governor's daughter there.

There was a little annunciator bell over the front door of the tobacco shop, and it rang merrily when she opened.

"I'll be right with you," a woman's voice called from

the shadows at the rear of the store. Sally Spengler had been in back of the shop, and she hurried forward now with a practiced smile on her face. The smile left when she saw that it was Fancy.

"Oh, it's you. What can I do for you, Miss Delight?" The question was without warmth.

Sally considered Fancy a fallen woman because of where she worked. She knew that Fancy and Amber had become friends, and though she had no right to criticize, it wasn't a friendship she encouraged. She believed that the immorality of Fancy's lifestyle couldn't help but have a detrimental effect on Amber.

On the other hand, she knew that Fancy and Amber were about the same age, and young women needed friends their own age. This would be especially true if one was virtually a prisoner, as Amber was. For that reason, Sally didn't speak against the young women's relationship, but she did treat Fancy with cool politeness.

"Miss Spengler, is Amber here? I must speak to her," Fancy said. "It is urgent."

Hearing the conversation out front, Clem Spengler came up from the back as well. When he saw Fancy, his smile was genuine and his words warm. Fancy was a very pretty girl, and though Clem's fidelity to his wife was inviolate, he was a man, after all, and he did enjoy looking at pretty women.

"Hello, Miss Delight," Clem said.

"Clem, she is looking for Amber," Sally said. "She says it is very urgent."

The smile left Clem's face. "What is it? Is the girl in danger?"

"I don't know," Fancy said.

"Well you must know something, or you wouldn't be looking for her."

"Someone wants to see her."

"Who?"

From outside, they heard shouting.

"You fellas go over to the stable and look up in the hayloft!"

"We've looked up there twice already. So has Mills and Spivey. He ain't up there, or we would'a found him by now."

Clem walked to the front door and looked out onto the street. "There have been three different groups of them come in here already, looking for this Drago person," Clem said. "He's not here, but do you think that keeps them from looking?" He shook his head. "Not at all. They'll probably be in again."

He turned away from the front door and looked back at Fancy. The expression on Fancy's face was one of great apprehension.

"What is it, child?" Sally asked gently, a crack appearing in her veneer of reserve.

"That's who wants to talk to Amber," Fancy said quietly.

"Who wants to talk to her?" Clem asked. He pointed toward the street. "Are you talking about Cosgrove and those men out there?"

"No," Fancy said. "Not them. The man they are looking for. That's who wants to talk to Amber."

"Drago?"

Fancy nodded.

"Good heavens, girl, you wouldn't send Amber to him! Not with the entire town looking for him. Why, she could get killed," Sally said.

"Do you know where he is?" Clem asked.

Fancy shook her head. "No. Not at this minute."

"But you have spoken to him?"

"Yes."

"Since he killed Barnes?"

"I was with him when he killed Barnes," Fancy said.

"That's all the more reason Amber shouldn't talk to him. He's a murderer."

"No he isn't," Fancy defended. "He didn't have any choice. Barnes was going to kill him. It was a fair fight. Barnes drew first."

"Yeah, that's what I've heard," Clem said. "They also say this Drago fella is faster than greased lightning. Who is he, anyway? And why would a gun-fighting outlaw want to speak with Amber?"

"He's not an outlaw," Fancy said. "He's a lawman. He has come here to help us."

"How can one man help us?" Sally asked.

"He's not an ordinary man," Fancy replied.

"I can believe that. Anyone who could shoot down Barnes in a fair fight is anything but ordinary," Clem said.

"No, I don't mean that. I mean he is . . ." Fancy didn't know how to explain what she meant. The man they all knew as Drago did not outdraw Barnes, at least, not in the classic sense. But, somehow, the gun appeared in his hand and then, just as mysteriously, it disappeared. She had been sitting at the table with him, but she didn't know how that had happened.

She was also unable to describe a person who could so drastically change his appearance that she couldn't recognize him even though he told her who he was. And what words, other than "ghost," could she use to tell how, as she was leaving her house, he stood before her one moment, but completely disappeared in the next?

"What do you mean?" Clem asked.

"He is . . . different," Fancy said. It was the only way she could think of to describe him.

14

On the evening of the day of the first balloon ascension and Billy Bates's parachute leap, Professor Thomas accepted an invitation from Jim to have dinner in Jim's private car.

Thomas listened to music on Jim's Edison Machine, and looked at pictures through the stereoscope. Then, as they waited for their meal to be served, they played a game of billiards.

"I must say, Mr. West, this is the most amazing conveyance I have ever seen," Thomas said. "To think that one could travel all over the country in such luxury. Thank you very much for inviting me to see it, and to have dinner with you."

"Would you like some more wine, Professor?" Jim offered.

"Yes, dear boy, thank you," Thomas said, holding out his glass.

"How does it work?" Jim asked as he poured the wine.

"I beg your pardon?"

"The balloon," Jim said. "What does one need to know to fly it?"

Professor Thomas laughed. "Oh, I can scarcely tell you in a few words what it has taken a century of scientific experimentation to develop," he answered.

"Try," Jim suggested.

"Very well. The most important thing to keep in mind is balance. Balance and ballast," Thomas said. "What one does is fill the envelope with lifting gas that one gets from the gas generator. Once the balloon has sufficient lift, it is safe to go aloft. Allow the balloon to rise until it finds its own altitude. There, the balloon will float, as a cork does on water. If you wish to go higher, throw over some ballast. If you wish to go lower, release some gas."

"How did you know where to send the wagon to retrieve you?" Jim asked as he poured the talkative professor more wine. "Is the balloon not subject to the vagaries of wind?"

"Yes, of course it is," Thomas replied. He held up his finger. "But is a sailing ship not also dependant upon the wind? And yet the world holds no secrets from the intrepid explorations of man, because we have learned to master those varying winds which propel our ships across the sea."

"That is true," Jim agreed.

"And, as ship's pilots have learned to steer their vessels along any course, regardless of the direction of the wind, so too shall we discover how to make aerostats obey our will."

"And you did that today?"

Thomas laughed. "Not entirely," he admitted. He poured himself another drink. "That's just what I tell people. The truth is, I always know the direction of the winds, both on the ground and aloft, for they are not always the same. And I can maneuver the balloon up or down until I find a strata of wind blowing in the direction I want to go."

"And what about the parachute leap the boy made?"

"Thrilling, wasn't it?"

"Yes."

"Thank God for the boy. If he hadn't come forward when he had, this would have been a wasted day. Up until the boy agreed to make the leap, I had earned only eight dollars. But I was able to raise more than a hundred at the prospect of someone leaping to their death."

"Leaping to their death?"

Thomas laughed. "Well, I think there is a morbid streak deep inside everyone. Some of the spectators today were secretly hoping that the boy would fall to his death. That is why I was able to raise as much money as I did. The really ironic thing is that the stunt the boy did, though exciting, is scarcely more dangerous than crossing the street and risking being hit by a runaway team."

"I didn't realize that."

"Most don't," Thomas said. "That's why they are so willing to pay to see it. Don't get me wrong; it takes a lot of courage to step over the edge of the gondola when the ground is six hundred feet down. Intellectually, I know that it isn't dangerous. But psychologically, I am quite unable to do it."

"Professor, I want to hire your balloon," Jim said.

"Hire it, sir? You mean you wish to make an ascension?"

"More than that. I want to hire it for my exclusive use," Jim said.

"I can't do that," Thomas said. "I will lose too much money."

"I will pay you two hundred dollars for the exclusive use of your balloon."

"Two hundred dollars? That is a lot of money."

"Yes," Jim said. "Have we a bargain?"

Professor Thomas grinned happily. "For two hundred dollars, I will take you anywhere you wish to go. When do you want to start?"

"We will begin tomorrow. I want to make an ascension with you, just to see how things work."

"Very well. I will have the balloon inflated and ready to lift by ten o'clock in the morning," Thomas said. With the one hundred dollars he had made that day, and the two hundred he would be getting from Mr. West, this had turned into quite a profitable stop for him.

When Jim approached the wicker basket the following morning, Professor Thomas gave him a fur cap and a fur muffler.

"You will need these," he said.

Jim waved them aside. "I'll be all right," he said. "It's actually quite warm."

Thomas smiled. "My dear friend, were it the hottest day of the year you would need these items, for today we shall ascend to a height of ten thousand feet. At that altitude it gets very cold."

"Very well," Jim said. "In that case, thank you. I will take them." He took the proffered items, then as a few of the good people held the gondola steady, he climbed over the railing. Thomas climbed in right behind him.

"In the event that I become incapacitated for some reason, pull this cord," Thomas explained, pointing to the balloon rip cord.

"What will that do?"

"This is called a rip cord because pulling on it will rip open a panel and allow the gas to escape. That will cause the balloon to descend."

"What would keep the balloon from falling like a rock?"

Thomas laughed. "Not to worry, Mr. West. The gas will not be able to escape so quickly as to allow a too-rapid descent." He pointed to where he wanted Jim to be, and Jim moved into position.

Thomas began calling out orders to the ground crew he had recruited just for this purpose. Ropes were released, and the balloon began to rise.

At first Jim thought it was rising slowly, though he was amazed at how quickly he found himself looking down first at the buildings of Phoenix, and then at the highest trees. As the balloon drifted higher still, he could see the entire town from edge to edge, and he could also see the tracks running south from the town, stretching almost endlessly out into the desert.

"How high are we now?" Jim asked.

Professor Thomas inspected the barometer, then made a few calculations.

"At the time of my checking, we were at five hundred feet," he said. "But I expect we are over six hundred now."

They gained more altitude, and Jim saw that he was

looking down on Camelback Mountain. A few moments later, Thomas checked the barometer again.

"We are two thousand feet high," he said.

From this altitude, Jim could see where the tracks curved, south of the town. He knew that was ten miles away.

"Five thousand feet," Thomas announced a few minutes later.

The town of Phoenix was now quite small. He was also surprised to see that it was some distance to the west of them. He had not been aware of any lateral motion.

"Seven thousand, five hundred," Thomas said.

The wicker-basket gondola continued to be borne aloft in a broad blue sky laced with cirrus clouds. True to Thomas's prediction, it became much, much colder, and Jim welcomed the fur hat and muffler that Thomas had insisted he bring. It was worth the discomfort, though, for the view from up here was more breathtaking than anything Jim had ever seen or imagined. For the first time in his life he could visualize Earth as round, because from horizon to horizon he could see the suggestion of a dipping curve.

Jim was suddenly startled by a hissing sound, and he quickly looked around to see Thomas opening a valve.

"What are you doing?" Jim asked.

"I am venting gas," the aeronaut explained. "We have reached the altitude of ten thousand feet. If we go much higher, we will run out of air and die of asphyxiation."

From this altitude, Jim could see where the railroad from Phoenix connected with the Southern Pacific. He could also see several towns along the tracks, including Ristine.

And he could see the Santa Estrella Mountains. He pointed to them.

"How could we get to those mountains?" he asked.

"They are southwest of our present position, and we are drifting northeast. That would make it difficult."

"Then you are saying it can't be done?"

Professor Thomas smiled. "My boy, I said it was difficult, but I didn't say it was impossible. As we passed through the altitude of about three thousand feet, I noticed that the wind was blowing in that direction. What one would have to do is maintain the level at which the wind is favorable to the direction you want to go."

"Three thousand feet? But the mountains are taller than three thousand feet, aren't they?"

"I'd say the tallest is about forty-five hundred feet."

"Suppose you wanted to land in the valley within the ring of those mountains—how would you do it?"

Thomas laughed. "Ah, testing my navigational skills, are you?"

"I was just interested, that's all," Jim said.

"Well, if I wanted to land in the valley, I would first ascertain the altitude at which the winds propelled me in the direction I needed to go. Then, as I drew closer, I would have to climb to a high enough altitude to enable me to clear the peaks. At the higher altitudes, the winds invariably blow from southwest to northeast, so I would probably have to go to the other side of the mountains, and then come back. Finally, it would be a simple matter of finding favorable winds by ascending or descending until such winds were encountered, in order to position me over the valley. Then I would vent enough gas to allow me to descend to the valley floor. But I wouldn't try it."

"Why not?"

"In order to be certain that you clear the mountains while looking for favorable winds, it might be necessary to climb even higher than we are now. Should you climb higher than fifteen thousand feet, you would die for lack of air."

Looking around in the gondola, Jim found a pair of binoculars. He raised this to his eyes, then studied the mountains.

"Tell me, Mr. West. What is it about those mountains that holds your fascination?" Professor Thomas asked.

"I'm just curious," Jim answered. He put the binoculars away.

Thomas vented more gas, and they began to descend.

"Look down there," Thomas said. "Do you see the wagon, come to meet us?"

"It's going to be a long walk," Jim said. "He looks as if he is at least ten miles away."

Thomas smiled. "Oh, were we to go straight down from here, it would be. But, watch this, my boy," he said.

For the next several minutes Professor Thomas alternated between venting gas—closing the valve to remain stationary—and throwing over ballast to rise. As he did so, Jim saw that they were actually moving toward the wagon.

"Amazing," Jim said. "We are getting closer."

"It's all a matter of finding favorable winds," Thomas said as he continued working. "And that is all a matter of finding the correct altitudes, or, what I like to call flight levels, since, with the aid of the wind we are, in effect, flying, and not just going up and down."

"Professor, once you touch down, would it be possible to go back up again immediately?"

"You mean without replacing the expended gas?"

"Yes."

"It depends on how much ballast you carried aloft during your first ascent. If you carried enough ballast, you could, after the flight, jettison all, or most of it, and the balloon would ascend once more, provided you were judicious in the venting of gas. You would be somewhat limited in your ability to navigate, however, for your only means of altitude control then would be in the venting of gas to come back down, and each time you descended, you would be unable to climb back up. My boy, we are here," he concluded.

Thomas pulled the rip cord and allowed the rest of the gas to escape, just as they touched down. The recovery wagon, which had been some ten miles distant when Jim first saw it, was now less than a quarter of a mile away, and was already coming for them.

With most of the gas gone, the envelope fell to one side, then slowly deflated until it was nothing but a bundle of silk.

In his private car that night, Jim took out a map of Arizona and began studying it. This was a particularly detailed map, with all the topographical features including the height of all the mountains in the Santa Estrella range.

Jim wrote the letter A on the map, which he indicated as the point of launch. He then drew a line to the southwest, to a point beyond the Santa Estrella range. There, he wrote the letter B, which he called the "Turn Around

Point." From B, he drew a shorter line to a place over the valley in the middle of the range of mountains. This he called C, and he labled it as the "Landing and Re-launch Point." From there, he drew another line right back to his original launch point, thus closing the triangle.

When he was finished, he put his pencil down, then leaned back and tapped his fingers on the desk. To make this work, the balloon would have to fly to a point inside the Santa Estrella range, land with the necessary assault equipment on board the balloon, make contact with Artie, find Amber, put her in the balloon, and bring her out. Once Amber was safely away, he and Artie would then be able to start their war with Cosgrove.

Did such a plan have a chance of success?

The first step in the success of any plan, Jim knew, was to identify the problem areas. If the problems could be identified, it might be possible to eliminate them.

And the first problem, as Jim saw it, was that of communication. To improve greatly the chances of success, Artie would have to be informed of the details in advance. But how was that to be accomplished? There were no telegraph wires into Presidio. There was no train, no stage, and from what he had been able to ascertain, no longer any mail, other than the mail that Cosgrove allowed through.

Jim recalled his meeting with Sheriff Walt in the governor's office.

"Communicatin' with him, now, that's goin' to be a problem," the sheriff had said. *"Unless you've got a trained pigeon. 'Cause 'bout the only way a body is goin' to get in there is fly."*

Jim smiled. Trained pigeon, huh? Well, he didn't have

a trained pigeon. But he had something better. He knew exactly how he was going to deliver the message.

"Jim, my boy," he said aloud. "You are a genius. An absolute genius."

He poured himself another glass of wine, then chuckled. He knew that Artie would tell him not to get the big head until the plan had succeeded. But Artie wasn't here, and Jim allowed himself a degree of what he considered to be justifiable pride.

15

Because the men guarding the pass swore that no one had left town that day, Cosgrove was certain that his quarry was still somewhere within the town—and certainly within the valley. He doubled the guard at the entrance to the pass just to make certain that Gordon couldn't sneak out after dark. He also put a watch on the horse Drago had ridden into town, thus limiting his access to the valley. If Gordon was here, he would find him. And he was pretty sure Gordon was still somewhere in the town.

To facilitate the search, Cosgrove put a one-thousand dollar reward on Gordon—dead.

"None of this dead or alive business," he said when he announced the reward. "I want him dead, dead, dead."

The promise of one thousand dollars was enough money to inspire even the most timid of Cosgrove's men. It also attracted a few of the more disreputable citizens of the town itself—men who had not openly joined Cosgrove's gang, but who had more in common with him than they did with the decent folk of the town.

The search that had begun in the early afternoon was still going on, now with more participants than ever. The problem was that Presidio was a very small town, and every place that could be searched *had* been searched. That didn't stop the searchers, though. They were after the money and not one commercial building or residence was spared the unwarranted invasion of private property. In fact, all had already been gone through more than once, and some had been subjected to half a dozen or more searches. Often, a new search crew would be waiting outside to start again, as soon as the old search was finished.

The first home owner whose house had been invaded had demanded a search warrant, but the searchers had merely laughed at his suggestion. No one ever mentioned it again after that.

Midway through the afternoon, someone happened to remember that the last time anyone had seen ''Drago'', he was sitting at a table with Fancy. Fancy was questioned several times to see if she could shed any light on Gordon's whereabouts, but she was, legitimately, in the dark about it. Her house was the most frequently searched building in the entire town.

As Amber walked down the street of the little town that evening, the town was literally buzzing with the hunt for Artemis Gordon. In front of her, behind her, and to either side of her, two- and three-man search teams looked high and low for Artemis Gordon. In most cases, one two-man team would be searching a place, while a second team waited for them to finish so that they could search the same place.

Aware of the intensity of the search, Amber thought it was a foolish waste of time for her to go to the City Pig to keep an appointment with the man Fancy said was here to rescue her. Surely he wouldn't be there. How could he be, with the entire town looking for him? And even if he was there, how could he rescue her? He would be doing well to rescue himself.

But Fancy insisted that Artemis Gordon was no ordinary man.

"If he says he will be there at seven o'clock, he will be there at seven o'clock," she said. "I don't know how he will be able to do this—but he will be there."

Taking Fancy at her word, Amber arrived at the City Pig at exactly seven o'clock.

The dining room was scented with the aroma of roast pork, baked apples, and cinnamon. Diners were at two of the tables and a waiter was standing by the counter to see to their needs. In the middle of the room, an old Mexican was sweeping the floor.

Just as she got inside, two of Cosgrove's men, Tyson and Davidson, pushed in behind her.

"Out of the way," Tyson demanded gruffly.

Quickly, Amber stepped to one side.

"Everybody stand up! Back up against the wall!" Tyson ordered, gruffly.

Lambert, the restaurant owner, came hurrying out of the kitchen. "See here, Tyson, this is the third time we have been searched within the last hour," he complained. "Can't you people leave us alone—at least during the dinner hour?"

"We're lookin' for a man named Artemis Gordon," Tyson said.

"Yes, yes, we know who you are looking for. The entire town knows who you are looking for," Lambert complained. "But if you haven't been able to find him in here after all the times we have been searched, don't you think he may just not be here?"

"We're not takin' any chances," Tyson said. "Davidson, you look in the kitchen. I'll keep an eye on these people out here."

"Right," Davidson answered, pushing open the kitchen door and looking inside. As Davidson was searching through the kitchen, Spivey and Mills came in from the alley, through the back door.

"See anything back there?" Davidson asked.

"Nobody out back," Spivey replied. "We searched the privy and the shed, too."

"What about the pantry?" Mills asked. "Have you looked in there?"

Although Davidson had looked in there during an earlier search of the kitchen no more than an hour ago, he shook his head no.

"Haven't looked in there, yet," Davidson answered.

"What do you say we have us a look-see?" Mills suggested.

With guns drawn, the three men pushed open the pantry door. Another team had been in here only fifteen minutes earlier, so all the goods stored in the pantry had been pulled away from the wall so that the searchers could see behind.

"What about that?" Davidson asked, pointing to a barrel. "I'll bet nobody's looked in there."

"That's the flour barrel," Spivey said.

"So, he could be down inside," Davidson insisted.

Davidson opened the lid, leaned over the barrel, then ran his hand down through the soft, sifted flour. When he raised it up again, he was covered with white dust. Mills laughed.

"What's so funny?" Davidson asked.

Mills pointed. "You. You're white as a ghost," he said, laughing again.

Davidson tried to brush some of the flour off, but he just spread it around. As a result, when the three of them stepped back into the dining room, he was practically covered with it.

"Oh, no," Lambert groaned. "Not my flour."

The others in the café laughed, including Amber.

"Nobody back there," Davidson said.

At that moment Pike and Kitridge came in through the front door, so now there were nearly as many searchers in the dining room as there were customers and employees of the restaurant.

"What happened to you?" Pike asked Davidson.

Davidson made another futile attempt to brush the flour away.

"Nothin'," he mumbled.

The customers and employees were still lined up against a wall, watching in frustrated anger as the searchers tried to determine what to do next.

"Our supper's getting cold," one of the diners said. "Can't we get back to our meal?"

"There ain't none of you goin' nowhere 'till we check ever'thing out," Tyson growled.

"You *have* checked everything," Lambert said. He pointed to the others, in turn. "And you have, and so have you. You were all in here half an hour ago, and you will probably be in here in another half hour. Can't you at least let my customers eat in peace?''

"Not until I take a good look at them," Tyson said.

He stepped up to the wall and stared at each of them.

"Tyson, I'm Bill Peters. I own the leather shop, for God's sake," one of the customers said. "You know who I am. You bought a saddle from me.''

"Could be," Tyson said. "But they say this fella can look like anyone.''

"Well if he can, he'd be dumb to look like someone as ugly as I am," Peters growled.

The others in the dining room laughed.

Tyson was the only one who didn't laugh. He stared long and hard at each man present, making them uncomfortable with the intensity of his stare.

Only the old Mexican, who stood over in the corner to maintain a respectable distance from the paying customers, and with his head down in humility, was spared Tyson's scrutiny.

"Come on, Tyson, he isn't in here," Pike said.

With a frustrated growl, Tyson agreed and all the searchers started to leave. Just as they started out the door, Tyson turned back to call out to Lambert and his customers, who were just returning to their tables.

"I know Gordon is still in town, somewhere," he said. "And if any of you are hiding him, it's going to be hard—very hard for you.''

The searchers left and the diners exhaled in unison, almost as if they had been holding their breath for the whole time.

"I wish they would hurry up and find that fella," one of the diners said. "Maybe we could have a little peace around here, then.''

"Who's peace?" Bill Peters asked. "Cosgrove's peace? I've had enough of his peace. They say this man Gordon is a federal lawman. I hope he gets away. I hope he is somewhere watchin' all this searchin' goin' on, and just laughin' his fool head off."

"Can I help you, Miss Morris?" Lambert asked, just now noticing Amber.

Amber looked around the café. Artemis Gordon obviously wasn't here, or Tyson and his bunch would have found him. She was tempted to leave, and she almost did so. But something held her here. Irrational as it might seem, Fancy had told her that Gordon was no ordinary man. And he was successfully avoiding the most thorough manhunt Amber had ever seen or imagined. If, at this point, he suddenly appeared in a puff of smoke, she wouldn't be too surprised.

"I . . . uh, would like a cup of coffee," she said.

"Yes, ma'am, I'll get it right away," Lambert said. "Oh, and you," Lambert said to the Mexican. "I suppose you've done enough work to earn a meal, by now. Have a seat; I'll bring you something to eat."

"Gracias, señor,*"* the old Mexican said. He took a seat at a table next to the table where Amber was sitting. He looked at Amber.

"Buenas noches, señor,*"* Amber said, somewhat disarmed by his unabashed stare at her.

"Buenas noches. You have ordered a cup of coffee, Señorita Morris. You might . . . fancy . . . some pie, as well," the old Mexican said quietly, setting the word "fancy" apart from the rest of the sentence.

"I might what?" Amber gasped. She might *fancy* some pie? Fancy? Was this merely coincidence? Or was the Mexican sending her a message? She decided that it was a message. It had to be. Artemis Gordon was hiding somewhere, and he sent this Mexican to take a message for him.

"You know, don't you?" she said under her breath. "You know where he is."

"*Si.*" The Mexican's answer was barely more than a whisper.

"Where is he? No, no, I don't want to know," she said quickly. "If I don't know, I can't inadvertently give him away."

The Mexican continued to look directly at her, affording her the opportunity of staring deep into his eyes. There was something about his eyes that disturbed her, and it took her a moment to realize that she had seen these same eyes somewhere before.

Suddenly she realized where she had seen them!

When the outlaw Drago first rode into town, she had been standing on the balcony, looking down. Drago had looked at her with those same deep eyes. Now she knew that Drago wasn't an outlaw, but was a federal lawman who was working in disguise. Just as she now knew that this wasn't an old Mexican, earning a meal by sweeping the floor. This was Artemis Gordon. Fancy had told her that he was no ordinary man, and now she could agree.

"You—" she started, but he made an almost imperceptible shake of his head, then put his finger to his lips to silence her.

"Thank you for coming," Artie said. As before, he spoke just loudly enough for her alone to hear him.

"I . . . I didn't know if you would be here," Amber said.

Artie smiled. "Oh, but I'm not here. They have searched several times and come up empty each time."

Lambert came from the kitchen then, carrying a plate in one hand and a cup of coffee in the other. He put the plate on the table in front of Artie, and the coffee in front of Amber.

"*Graçias,* señor," Artie said.

It was amazing, Amber thought as she watched him interact with Lambert. It wasn't just the disguise. Somehow this person had the ability to change his entire being. Now, as he groveled before the café owner, he *was* a Mexican peon.

When Lambert left, his personality changed again. Though he was still in the disguise of an itinerant old Mexican, his inner personality was one of poise and confidence.

"We are going to get you out of here," Artie said as he transferred a spoonful of beans to his mouth.

"We?"

"My partner and I."

"Then there is someone else in here, working with you?"

"Not yet. He will come."

"How? You came in through the pass. You saw how narrow it is, and how well-guarded. An army couldn't get through there."

"He'll be here," Artie said resolutely. "And when he comes, you must be ready to act."

"What do you want me to do?"

"Whatever we tell you to do," Artie said. "The important thing is, you must be ready to do it at once."

"I'll be ready," Amber said.

"Hey, you, Mex!" Lambert suddenly called. "Are you bothering Miss Morris?"

"Forgive me, señor," Artie said quickly, once more

assuming the persona of an underling. "I was telling the señorita about my children and how they do not always get enough to eat."

"I thought so! You were askin' her for money, weren't you?" Lambert growled angrily. He pointed to the door. "I won't have anyone panhandlin' in here. Get out!"

"But, señor, my dinner. I have not yet—"

"I told you, you could work for your dinner and have it, as long as you didn't bother any of my customers."

"Please, Mr. Lambert, it was my fault," Amber said. "Let him finish his supper."

Artie dipped his head slightly toward Amber in a bow. "*Gracias,* señorita. You are so kind," he said.

Lambert stroked his chin. "All right, you can finish your supper, then I want you out of here, do you understand?"

"*Si,* señor."

"No more askin' people for money. In fact, you just sit there and keep quiet and eat."

"*Si,* señor."

At that moment, Kitridge and another man came into the café.

"All right," Kitridge shouted. "We're lookin' for Artemis Gordon. Has anyone seen him?"

"Not again," Lambert complained.

"Yeah, again," Kitridge said. He pointed to the kitchen. "Jake, you check in there."

"Well, I don't have to go through this again," one of the diners said, getting up from his table and throwing his napkin on his plate. "A man can't even eat his dinner in peace without a bunch of ruffians coming in and searching for a ghost."

164

"Who says he is a ghost?" Kitridge asked.

"He must be," the diner replied. "The whole town has been looking for him all day long and no one has seen hide nor hair of him."

"He'll turn up," Kitridge said. "If you want my opinion, he's probably hidin' out somewhere, behind a privy, or in a watering trough. But I figure he's goin' to have to get hungry, and when he does, this is where he'll have to come for some grub."

"What a brilliant deduction," Lambert said dryly. "Did you come up with that all by yourself? Or did you just stand outside and watch everyone else come in here? Because you are about the one thousandth person to search in here. And he *ain't here!*" Lambert shouted the last two words.

Amber saw Artemis Gordon get up from the table and shuffle over to Kitridge. She remembered that Kitridge was one of the men who had brought Artie into town a few days ago, when Artie was disguised as Drago. Would Kitridge recognize him? It seemed a terrible risk and a foolish thing for Mr. Gordon to do, and yet, even as she watched, she knew that there was no danger of Kitridge recognizing him. If she blinked her eyes, she would almost be willing to say that this was a different person, even from the one she had just been speaking to.

"I beg your pardon, señor," Artie said. "May I go? I must find a place to sleep tonight."

Kitridge looked at Artie and snorted. There wasn't the slightest hint of recognition in his eyes. "You're lookin' for a place to sleep, are you, Mex?"

"*Si*, señor."

Kitridge pointed. "You might try the last house up at

the end of the street, on the left-hand side. They got a pigpen in the back. They might let you sleep there.''

Artie nodded in defeat. ''*Si*, señor,'' he mumbled self-consciously as he walked out the door and into the night.

Kitridge laughed out loud. ''Sleepin' in the pigpen,'' he said. ''That's a good place for a no-count Mexican like that.''

Jake came back from the kitchen. ''No one in there, Kitridge,'' he said.

''All right,'' Kitridge said. ''Let's go.''

Amber left immediately after Jake and Kitridge had left. She looked up and down the street for Artemis Gordon, but she didn't see him. She saw only those who were hunting for him. It had been only a few seconds since he had left. Where had he gone so quickly?

As three of the hunters walked by her, with guns drawn, one of them looked over and nodded. Amber started to turn away from him, to show her disdain for him and his kind. At the last minute, however, she caught a glimpse of his eyes—those dark, deep, expressive eyes.

Amber gasped. This was not the shuffling Mexican, nor was it the frightening Drago. This was a totally different person, a minor member of Cosgrove's outlaw gang, perhaps, or maybe a wrangler or one of the townspeople, out for a share of the reward money by finding Artemis Gordon.

But Amber knew, in that one flash of insight, that this would-be hunter was just another personification of Artemis Gordon.

Concealing a knowing smile, she nodded back at him.

16

As Billy Bates sucked up the last of the brown-colored liquid through a straw, it made a slurping noise in the bottom of the tall glass.

"What did you say this was, Mr. West?" he asked.

"A chocolate ice-cream soda," Jim answered.

Unable to get any more with the straw, Billy laid it aside, then turned the glass up for the last few drops. When he finished he had a small chocolate mustache, which he licked off with his tongue.

"It sure was good," Billy said. "Thanks. And thanks for inviting me in to see your train. I been wantin' to see it ever since it come here."

"Well, it was the least I could do for the young man who gave us all a thrill by making that parachute leap the other day."

Billy grinned broadly. "You seen me do that?"

"Indeed I did. I was in the crowd with the others," Jim said.

"That was the most fun I ever had in my life," Billy said.

"Was it enough fun that you would consider doing it again?"

"Yes, sir, you bet I would. I would do it in a heartbeat."

"Would you do it from higher up? Higher, say, than the balloon could be tethered?"

"You mean from a balloon that's just floatin' free? Yes, sir, I don't see why not. Seems to me the only difference is, it would take you a little longer to get to the ground, is all. I think I'd like to do it that way."

"What about at night? Would you do it at night?"

Billy looked at Jim with a puzzled expression on his face.

"Mr. West, you're gettin' at somethin' here, ain't you?"

"I might be," Jim admitted. "How old are you?"

"I'm fifteen, goin' on sixteen," Billy answered resolutely.

"Did you know that during the great Civil War there were lots of young men, no older than you, who fought for their country?"

"Yes, sir, I know'd that. My pa, he was one," Billy said. "He fought at Antietam when he was only twelve. He was a drummer boy. Sometimes I wish there was a war so I could fight."

"Oh?"

"Well, not really," Billy amended quickly. "I mean, I know wars are terrible things, what with lots of folks getting killed and all. But if there was one goin' on, I'd sure be wantin' to get in it.''

"I understand,'' Jim said. "What you are saying is, you sometimes wish you had the opportunity to do some service for your country.''

"Yeah, that too,'' Billy said. "As long as it was somethin' exciting,'' he added.

"Billy, do you know what the Secret Service is?''

"No, sir, I don't. Is it somethin' secret?''

Jim laughed. "In a manner of speaking, it is,'' he said. "It is an agency of the United States Government. I work for them as a lawman.''

"Like a sheriff?''

"More like a U.S. Marshal, actually. You see, I don't take my orders from the town, or the county. I work directly for the president of the United States.''

"Wow!'' Billy said. "That must really be exciting.''

"It is, sometimes,'' Jim said.

"How does a fella go about gettin' a job like that?'' Billy asked.

Jim chuckled. "Funny you should ask that. What if I told you that there was an opportunity for you to do something like that—to perform a service for the president of the United States? It would be exciting. In fact, it would be downright dangerous. But it would also pay you two hundred dollars. Would you be interested?''

"Two hundred dollars?'' Billy exclaimed, gasping at the amount of money. "You mean I could do somethin' exciting' like that, and earn two hundred dollars? Yes, sir, I'd be mighty interested.''

"I thought you would be,'' Jim said. "At least, I hoped so.''

"Wait a minute. Does this have anything to do with

what you were asking me a few minutes ago? Is this about making a parachute leap at night?''

"From a great height, yes.''

"Well, now, that don't make no sense, a'tall, Mr. West. If I make a parachute leap at night, there won't nobody be able to see it. Especially what with the parachute being black an' all.''

"That's good,'' Jim said. "We don't want anyone to see you.''

"We don't? Then I don't understand. If nobody can see me make the parachute leap, then there ain't nobody goin' to pay any money. How are we goin' to make that two hundred dollars you was talkin' about?''

"You don't worry about the two hundred dollars, Billy. I'll pay that,'' Jim said. "You aren't going to be jumping for the public. You are going to be jumping for the president of the United States.''

"I am? What do you think of that!'' Billy said, excited now by the prospect.

"Can you read a map?''

"Yes, sir, somewhat, I can. I can tell about mountains and towns and roads and railroads and such.''

Jim pulled the map he had been working on out of its cubbyhole, then unrolled it. He had to weight the corners down to keep them from curling back. He pointed to the triangle he had drawn earlier.

"Do you see this mountain range?'' Jim asked, pointing to the map. "It's called the Estrella range.''

"Yes, sir, I know about them mountains. They are down that way a mite.'' Billy pointed to the south. "I seen 'em from a distance, last time I hopped a ride on a freight train headin' south.''

"Well, if you go along with this plan, you are going

to see them a lot closer," Jim said. "I want you to get into the balloon here at point A. We are then going to fly you south by southwest to point B. At point B, we will come west by northwest back along the line to point C. Point C is just on the other side of the mountains right in the middle of the Estrella ring, over the valley. I expect we will be somewhere over the valley then. That's where I want you to jump out of the balloon."

"That fella Cosgrove, the one that's been robbin' all the trains and everything is in there, ain't he?" Billy asked.

"Yes. That's why I want you to jump at night so nobody can see you."

"When I get in there, what do you want me to do?"

"I have a friend inside," Jim explained. "Another Secret Service agent. Of course, nobody inside knows he is a Secret Service agent. They think he is an outlaw like the rest of them. I want you to take a message to him."

"That's all? You just want me to deliver a message?"

"Yes."

Billy laughed and hit his fist in his hand. "Hot damn!" he said. "This here's like bein' a spy or somethin', ain't it?"

"Yes," Jim said.

"If I do this, am I a Secret Service agent, too?"

"You are for this job," Jim agreed.

"What do I do after I give the message?"

"All you have to do then is wait. Professor Thomas and I will come back with the balloon, land, and pick you and Miss Morris up, then take you out of there."

"Miss Morris? You mean the governor's daughter?"

"Yes."

"We're goin' in to rescue her?"

"Yes."

"Hot damn! Then I'd not only be a Secret Service agent, I'd be sort of a hero, too, wouldn't I?"

Jim smiled. "Yes, it would make you very much a hero," he said.

"When do we go?" Billy asked.

"You will make your parachute leap tonight," Jim said.

"Tonight?"

"If you agree to it. Billy, remember, I am asking you to volunteer for this job. If you would rather not do it, tell me now, and I won't think any the worse of you."

"This message that I'm takin' to your friend, what does it say?" Billy asked.

"It says I'm coming tomorrow night. He needs to know, so he can make certain that he has Miss Morris ready to leave. Otherwise it might not work."

"So, what I'm doin' is important?"

"Very important."

"What if I don't do it? Will you go tomorrow night anyway?"

"Yes. We'll just have to take our chances."

"No," Billy said.

Jim sighed, and nodded. "I understand, and like I said, I don't think any less of you."

"No, sir, you don't understand," Billy said. "I mean no, you won't have to take your chances. I'll deliver the message for you."

Jim grinned broadly, then reached out to shake Billy's hand.

"You are a brave and noble young man," he said.

"I just need to tell my mom."

"All right. Be back after dark."

Billy started to leave, then he paused. "On second thought, it's probably not such a good idea to tell my mom," he said. "She won't understand, and she'll just try and talk me out of it. It's best she not know anything about it until it's all over."

Jim nodded. "You're beginning to grow up, Billy," he said. He took out his billfold, then started extracting bills. "I don't want to frighten you anymore, but here are the two hundred dollars I promised you. It might be better for you to take it now—"

"In case I don't make it?" Billy finished. He grinned. "That don't frighten me anymore," he said. "A fella would have to be a fool not to know somethin' bad could happen. I'll just put it in an envelope and leave it where Mom can find it."

With Billy persuaded to do his part, it now fell upon Jim to convince Professor Thomas. Though Thomas was considerably older than Billy, Jim had the idea that some of the same strategy might work. After all, a man would not make a career of flying balloons unless he had a certain spirit of adventure about him. All Jim would have to do is appeal to that sense of adventure.

"Have I ever flown at night?" the professor repeated Jim's question. "Yes, I've flown at night."

"But how can you see at night? How do you know where to go?"

"If the moon is bright enough, as it is now that there is a full moon, you can see quite well, actually. Oh, you can't make out individual things on the ground—such as a wagon, or a man, or anything like that. But you can see mountains, trees, and desert quite well."

"Could you see well enough to do what I inquired about the other day?" Jim asked. "Could you navigate to, and then around, the Santa Estrella Mountains? And then, could you find the correct altitude to come back over them, so that the balloon is directly over the valley?"

Professor Thomas looked directly at Jim.

"What is this, Mr. West? You have been particularly fascinated with those mountains from the very beginning."

"I want to fly over those mountains tonight."

"Tonight?"

"Yes."

"All right. That will require some skilled navigational procedures, but I don't see why I can't accommodate you."

"There is one more thing," Jim said.

"What's that?"

"You know the boy, Billy Bates?"

"Ah, the young man who made the parachute leap," Professor Thomas said. "Brave lad, he is. Yes, I know him. What about him?"

"He is going to make a parachute leap tonight down into the valley, right in the middle of the Estrella ring of mountains."

"Have you gone mad?" Professor Thomas gasped. "What in heaven's name would you want to do such a thing as that for?"

"I will get to that later," Jim explained. "The question now, is, are your navigational skills equal to the task?"

"You mean can I deliver the boy to the spot where

he can make a parachute descent without fear of landing on top of one of the mountains?''

"That is exactly what I mean.''

"The answer is yes. I can do that,'' Thomas said. "But a parachute leap at night is more dangerous than one in the daytime. One can't see the ground coming up, and it is more difficult to gauge heights.''

"It can be done, can't it?''

"Oh, yes, it can, and it has been done, many times. The young woman who used to make parachute leaps for me often did so at night, carrying a torch with her on the way down. In that way, her descent could be tracked by those on the ground. It made for quite a thrilling show.''

"The boy won't be carrying a torch,'' Jim said. "I don't want anyone on the ground to see him.''

"This is all very unusual,'' Thomas said. "And again, I must warn you, it is dangerous.''

"I am counting on you to tell the boy all he needs to know to make it as safe as possible.''

"Yes, well, under the circumstances, I don't know how safe that will be. Is the boy aware of the danger?''

"I am sure that he is. But before we ascend, you may tell him again if you wish. I want Billy to be absolutely certain that he understands, fully, what he is getting into.''

"I'll tell him. Believe me, I'll tell him. It would be very bad for my business if someone got badly hurt, or even killed, in conjunction with my balloon.''

"Professor, I don't want to force him, or you, into this,'' Jim said. "But I will tell you that it is very important.''

Professor Thomas thought for just a moment, then he nodded.

"All right, Mr. West, you can explain everything to me . . ." he began. Then he smiled, "as we are filling the balloon with gas. If we are going tonight, then I must start getting ready now."

When Governor Morris lit the lantern in his living room, the light illuminated James West. Jim had been sitting in a chair in the dark, waiting for him.

The governor was so startled by Jim's unexpected appearance that he jumped and called out Jim's name.

"West!"

"I'm sorry if I startled you, Governor," Jim said. "But I didn't want to see you in your office, because what I have to say to you is for your ears only."

"You are welcome here, of course, Mr. West. But are you suggesting that there is no privacy in my office?"

"I am."

"But the walls are so thick. When the doors are closed, I don't see how any conversation could be compromised."

"Check your stove," Jim said. "With the grates open in your office, and open in Howard Parker's office, everything you say can be overheard."

"Lord!" Morris said. "I never even thought about such a thing."

"You aren't alone," Jim said. "I didn't think about it either, until tonight. Then I went over there to check it out. Parker knows everything, including the fact that Artie has infiltrated Cosgrove's group."

"And, his knowing that is dangerous?"

"What Parker knows, Cosgrove knows."

Morris pinched the bridge of his nose. "I thought he was my friend. I thought I could trust him."

"It's happened before, Governor. Even Caesar had his Brutus."

"Are you going to arrest him?"

Jim shook his head. "I'm after bigger fish," he said. "I leave Parker to you. But if you are going to do anything about it, I would suggest that you do it first thing in the morning."

"Something is up, isn't it?"

"Yes."

"What is it?" Morris held his hand up then, and shook his head. "No, no, don't tell me. I think it would be best that I don't know."

"I'll tell you this much," Jim said. "If we are successful, you'll have your daughter back within forty-eight hours."

"And if you aren't?"

Jim smiled, reassuringly. "That's an option I choose not to consider," he said.

"Whatever it is that you are doing, Mr. West, my prayers go with you. In the meantime, I will do my part. And as for Parker, I won't wait until morning. He'll be in jail within the hour."

17

Jim West and Professor Thomas worked in the dark to inflate the balloon. Jim had thought that their activity might draw a crowd of curious onlookers, but if anyone saw them out in Phoenix Park, he didn't come over to investigate. Perhaps it was because Professor Thomas had already been in Phoenix for a few days and had made several ascensions. Familiarity with the process had made people jaded to a degree. They considered the inflation of the balloon to be a routine thing. Those who did happen by merely assumed that the balloon was being inflated for an ascension the next day. And as the actual ascension was much more interesting to watch than the inflation, no one stopped to bother them.

Jim was glad they were alone. He didn't think anyone would be able to figure out what was going on. Nevertheless, he wanted to keep tonight's operation, and the one tomorrow night, as secret as possible.

Professor Thomas adjusted one of the valves for the hose that was pushing lifting gas from the generator into the balloon envelope. When he was certain that everything was going as it should, he stood back to monitor the inflation.

"Now, Mr. West. I believe you said you would explain, later? Why would you want the boy to make a parachute leap at night, and why is it important that the people on the ground not see him?"

Jim showed Professor Thomas his Secret Service badge, then, briefly, filled him in on Cosgrove and Cosgrove's criminal activities, to include occupying an entire town, and holding the governor's daughter as his captive. Jim concluded by telling Thomas that it was his mission to capture Cosgrove and free both the town and Miss Morris.

"You are expected to do all that by yourself?" Thomas asked.

"No, I have a partner," Jim answered. "He is already inside. But he needs to know that I'm coming tomorrow night, so he can make plans and be ready for me."

"I see," Thomas said. "So you are going to have the boy make a parachute leap down in the valley, just to inform your friend?"

"Yes. I'm sure you don't approve, but—"

Professor Thomas interrupted Jim with a whooping laughter.

"On the contrary, my dear boy, on the contrary," he said. "I do approve. You see, for years I have been trying to convince the United States Government that the balloon is a wonderful tool, with uses as yet not even imagined. To think that it would be a delivery vehicle for the first practical application of the parachute? Why, we could make history!''

"I'm glad you see it that way.''

"Of course I see it that way. I will maneuver the balloon with such care that the boy will be able to land right in the middle of the valley.''

Jim put his hand on the professor's shoulder. "Good for you, Professor,'' he said. "I hope you have the same enthusiasm for what I am going to ask you to do tomorrow night.''

"I think I already have it figured out,'' Thomas said. "You will make the parachute leap tomorrow night.''

Jim smiled. "Not quite. Tomorrow night I want you to land the balloon inside the Santa Estrella ring, let me off, then take on the boy and Miss Morris as passengers and lift off again.''

"Oh,'' Professor Thomas said. "Oh my, oh my. That will be quite a difficult feat.''

"Can you do it?''

"You understand, of course, that I will have to vent gas to land . . . and I will not be able to take on any more gas before I take off.''

"Yes.''

"It depends upon how much ballast I can make our initial ascension with,'' Thomas concluded. "Also, upon how much we have to throw overboard to navigate. If we still have enough ballast on board when we land to throw off sufficient weight to compensate for the loss of the gas we vent, and to accommodate the addition of two passengers to the one I shall lose, I may be able to do it.''

"I will have some weapons and equipment with me,'' Jim said. "I am sure that my weight, plus the weight of the weapons and equipment, will be greater than the total weight of the boy and woman."

"Yes," Thomas said. "That is true, isn't it? Well, now, this does make for a most interesting aeronautical problem. I shall spend tomorrow making all the mathematical computations necessary." Thomas smiled. "I look forward to it, Mr. West."

"Good evening, Mr. West, Professor Thomas," Billy said. His sudden appearance caught them by surprise, because he was dressed in black and didn't materialize from the darkness until he was nearly at the balloon. "I wore black," Billy said. "I thought it would help keep me from being seen."

"With a black balloon, a black parachute, and black clothing, you will be practically invisible," Jim said. He chuckled. "Though in truth, I don't think their guards would be on the lookout for anyone dropping down on them from above, anyway."

"No sir, I wouldn't think so," Billy said. "You know, Mr. West, I was thinking about this parachute leap. Don't you think this would be a good idea for the cavalry? They could send a whole bunch of balloons up into the air and drop parachute troopers down on the enemy from above."

"Parachute troopers," Thomas repeated, laughing. "That's another good idea for the practical application of balloons and parachutes. By golly, you two have given me much to think about."

"Billy, are you sure you are ready for this?" Jim asked. "Remember, it's not too late to back out."

"No, sir, I don't want to back out," Billy answered. "But there are some things I need to ask you. What is your friend's name? And what does he look like?"

"His name is Gordon. Artemis Gordon," Jim answered. "And, as for what he looks like, well, do you know what a chameleon is?"

Billy shook his head. "No, sir."

"A chameleon is a lizard," Professor Thomas explained. "But he is quite an amazing fellow. If you put him on a red surface, he will be red. If you put him on something green, then he will turn green."

"Why would he do somethin' like that?" Billy asked.

"So that he can hide from the predators who would attack him," Professor Thomas explained.

Billy looked at Jim with a puzzled expression on his face. "This here Gordon fella that I'm taking the message to—is he like them lizards? Does he change colors?"

Jim laughed. "In a manner of speaking, he does. You see, Artemis Gordon is a master of disguise. One never knows how he will appear, and I must confess that there have been times when even I have been fooled."

Billy sighed in frustration. "If that is true, Mr. West, then there is no way I can find him," he said.

"Don't worry about finding him," Jim said. "He will find you."

"How?"

"For one thing, Mr. Gordon was here in Phoenix for a few days, and he is a very observant man. If you delivered any messages to anyone during that time, he would have seen you. Thus, when he sees you inside Presidio, he will know that you are from here." Jim removed a pearl stickpin from his cravat. "And, if you are wearing this"—he pushed it through the collar of Billy's shirt—"he will know that I have sent you."

"All right, so what do I do?"

"You don't do anything. Artemis will find you, and he will make contact with you."

"Do you have a letter for me to deliver?"

"No," Jim replied. "Just tell him to have Miss Morris ready to leave, tomorrow night."

"What if someone else approaches me? How can I be sure I'm talking to the right person?"

Jim thought for a minute. "When Artemis approaches you, ask him how much he paid for his special bottle of brandy. No one else will know the answer."

"How much was it?"

"One hundred dollars."

Both Billy and Professor Thomas gasped.

"One hundred dollars?" Billy said. "You mean he paid that much money for something you drink?"

"It is a very special brandy, bottled exclusively for Napoleon Bonaparte," Jim explained. "Disgraceful, I know, but it is the kind of extravagance Mr. Gordon sometimes allows himself."

"With Mr. Gordon's chameleon-like abilities, his courage in sneaking into the stronghold of such villainous characters, coupled with his appreciation of some of life's finer things, he sounds like a most interesting fellow," Professor Thomas said.

"He is," Jim said. "One could not ask for a better partner, or a closer friend. And he is depending on me. You can see, then, why I will not let him down."

"Nor will we," Billy added dramatically.

"Gentlemen, it is time for us to put our resolve into motion," Professor Thomas announced. "For there is now sufficient lifting gas for us to begin our aerostation. Please climb into the wicker basket, and we shall be away."

Because there had been no one there to watch the inflation, there was also no one there to watch the ascension. That meant there was no one to help. Because of that, Professor Thomas had to disconnect the hose and untie the balloon mooring lines himself. As he did so, Jim and Billy climbed into the wicker basket. The balloon began to rise, even as Thomas started scrambling aboard, and Jim and Billy reached down to help pull him into the basket. The balloon was already several feet into the air by the time Thomas was inside.

As the balloon ascended, Jim observed a phenomenon that balloonists were well aware of, but that he had not noticed before. Because of the absolute silence of the flight, and the fact that sound travels upward, they were able to hear the disembodied conversations of several townspeople, coming up from the dark. Down below, cloaked by the night, and unaware of the black balloon rising above them, men and women engaged in conversations they thought were private.

"I told Eddie, if he didn't have that horse shoed for me by three o'clock tomorrow . . ." one man began.

"Mason and Peabody was both there, they seen it, you can ask. . . ." a second conversationalist said, completely unaware that his dialogue was interplaying with another, though half the town separated the two.

Still a third conversation disclosed even more personal words. "Lucy, I swear, you're the prettiest thing I ever seen. Why don't you and me . . ."

Billy giggled. "Listen," he said. "It's like standin' just underneath ever'one's window."

"Oh yes," Professor Thomas replied. "I have heard all sorts of the most private and scandalous conversations during my many ascensions. If people only knew."

185

Mercifully for the unsuspecting overheard townspeople, the balloon quickly passed out of the range of conversations. Soon after, even the louder noises of the town quieted as Phoenix's little cluster of brightly lit buildings seemed to slide to the east, on the ground below. Of course, the town wasn't going east, the balloon was going west; but since they had no feeling of any lateral motion, it was hard to tell.

"I have found the first layer of favorable winds for us," Thomas said as he vented gas to maintain what he called the "flight level."

Although Jim had always thought that balloon flights were no more controllable than dandelion seeds in the wind, Professor Thomas was providing a vivid demonstration of the possibilities of the craft. He made constant checks of the compass, the barometer, and his pocket watch. He also had an artillery-sighting instrument, by which he could judge distances. Using all the instruments at his disposal, he constantly manipulated the gas vents and ballast to position the balloon at the most opportune altitudes, all the while maintaining a lateral progression toward the mountains. Once, Thomas made some measurements with his artillery range finder, then declared that they were moving at a speed he judged to be approximately thirty-five miles per hour.

"Not as fast as the swiftest train, I admit," he said. "But then, there are no tracks up here, are there?"

They passed just to the north of the Santa Estrella Mountains, their direction of motion moving them to the southwest. Soon they had traveled completely over the mountains, which were now east by northeast of their position.

"Now," Thomas said, smiling. "There is always a good, steady, northeasterly flow at ten thousand feet. We will just climb to that level, then ride the wind."

Thomas tossed over several bags of ballast, and the balloon began climbing. At just over ninety-five hundred feet, the balloon stopped its southwesterly drift, then started back on an east by northeast line.

Jim had little to do during this voyage. He dropped ballast when Thomas ordered it done, and he talked quietly, calmly, to Billy, to keep the boy from thinking too much about the task before him. He also looked at the moon and the stars. He knew that he was not significantly closer to the heavenly bodies, at least, not in the overall scheme of things. But he didn't think he had ever seen the stars more brilliantly displayed, nor the moon shining more brightly.

So clear was their view of the moonlit desert and mountains below them that Jim began to fear that his plan would be compromised because the outlaws would be able to see them coming.

"I had no idea it would be this bright," Jim said as the balloon drifted swiftly toward its destination.

Thomas chuckled. "Don't worry about being seen, Mr. West," he said, as if reading Jim's mind. "We're quite invisible up here."

"I suppose so. Still, I am amazed by how clearly I can see things."

"That's because there is a great brightness coming up from the ground. It is the reflected light of the moon. The Earth's surface is like a great mirror, shining back with light. I have no way of proving it, of course, but I am certain that if one could take a balloon all the way to the moon, then Earth would be as bright an orb in the

187

moon's midnight sky as the moon is in ours.''

"Mr. West, I can see a town down in the valley,'' Billy said, pointing.

Jim picked up the binoculars and looked toward the little town that Billy had pointed out. It was after midnight, so, for the most part, the town was nothing but black cubes and squares against the valley floor. There were a couple of lights, and they shined all the brighter for their isolation.

"You'd better get ready, Billy,'' Thomas said.

"Are you sure? We are so far away,'' Billy answered.

"We are about three miles away,'' Thomas said. "But we are nearly two miles high. If you leap now, you will drift three miles toward the east and northeast before you hit the ground.''

"Oh,'' Billy said. "I didn't know that.''

"Billy, are you sure you want to go through with this?'' Jim asked. "It's still not too late for you to back out.''

"I'm going to do it,'' Billy said. "Why, I wouldn't miss this chance for all the tea in China.''

"All right, Billy, if you are going to do it, you need to get over here and let me hook you up,'' Professor Thomas said.

Responding to Professor Thomas's call, Billy stepped over to the side of the gondola, then held his arms out as the professor began affixing the straps to him. The straps were coming from a stovepipe apparatus that was mounted vertically alongside the gondola. Inside the tube was a carefully folded canopy of silk. It took Thomas but a moment to make all the connections, utilizing the buckles and snaps that made the fastening easier.

Finally Billy was securely tied and buckled to the parachute harness.

"Now?" Billy asked.

"Wait," Thomas answered. He picked up his artillery range finder and, looking through it, made an estimate of the distance. "Climb over the wicker of the basket and hold onto the support lines. When I give the word, push yourself away. Remember, your weight will pull the parachute free. All you have to do, then, is drift down as gently as a feather."

"Is there anything different about landing at night?" Billy asked. "Anything I should be on the lookout for?"

"Only thing I can think of is, don't look at the ground right beneath you. You should fix your gaze at a point about twenty or so yards in front of you, and measure your distance that way," Thomas explained. "If you look straight down, you will think you are staring into a dark and bottomless pit."

Billy nodded.

Thomas took one more look through his artillery range finder. For a moment, there was an eerie silence as Thomas stared through his sighting device while Jim and Billy stared at him. Then Thomas held up his hand.

"Now," he said, bringing his hand down, sharply.

Billy didn't say a word. Instead he just pushed himself away from the side of the wicker basket. For one instant it looked, to Jim, as if Billy were suspended in midair alongside them, a fellow traveler through space.

Then he disappeared as he dropped down out of sight.

Hurriedly, Jim stepped to the side of the gondola and looked down.

Billy had already disappeared from view. A moment later, Jim heard an unfamiliar popping sound.

"What was that?" Jim asked, anxiously.

Professor Thomas smiled.

"That was a sound we wanted to hear," he said. "That was the sound of his parachute opening."

18

Billy felt his stomach coming up to his throat as he fell. It was not an unexpected sensation; he had felt it when he had jumped the first time. It lasted for only a few seconds, however; then the parachute opened above him with a reassuring, rippling, popping sound. As the chute opened, he felt the opening shock transmitted through the suspension straps to his thighs, waist, and shoulders.

Although he was glad to hear it, it seemed much louder to him this time and he was afraid they may have heard it from the ground. If so, they might be tempted to look up, to see what it was. Could they see him, if they looked up?

Billy looked up toward the balloon. He made a thorough sweep of the midnight sky, but the balloon was nowhere to be seen.

Wait! There! For just a moment, Billy was positioned in such a way as to cause the balloon to be silhouetted against the bright, silver orb of the moon. It was for a moment only; then the balloon passed on and it was gone. Had it not been backlit by the moon, he would have seen absolutely nothing, even though he knew the balloon was there and he knew where to look.

That exercise made him feel a lot better. If he couldn't see the balloon, given that it was large and that he knew where to look, then there was no way anyone on the ground would be able to see him.

He looked straight down between his feet, and saw only blackness.

What was it Professor Thomas had said? Oh, yes, don't look straight down, or you will think you are suspended over a dark, bottomless pit.

Quickly, Billy looked out in front of him, glancing down at an angle of about forty-five degrees. To his relief the ground not only took on some texture, but he could actually see what it looked like. He saw several fairly good-sized boulders, and he prayed that he wouldn't land on one of them. To do so, he feared, could cause him to break an arm, or a leg.

The ground was coming up faster now, much more quickly, it seemed, than it had when he had made the first jump. He felt a momentary panic, wondering if perhaps the parachute wasn't working properly. Then he reasoned that it might just seem as if he was falling faster because it was dark and he couldn't see quite as well.

He *was* falling faster. At least it certainly felt that way when he hit the ground. This was a much harder landing than the other one had been. He fell, then rolled painfully along the ground, bruised by the rocks and stabbed by cactus needles.

When he stopped rolling, he lay there for a moment

just to gather himself. Slowly, painfully, he sat up. There was very little about his body that didn't ache, and yet he was also experiencing the most tremendous sense of exhilaration.

He had fallen from a balloon that was two miles high in the sky and except for a painful bruise or two, he was all right! He wanted to scream and shout with joy, but he knew that he should not.

Finally, Billy stood up and looked around. He had landed no more than one thousand yards from the edge of the town. He could be there with a walk of less than ten minutes.

He began unsnapping, unhooking, and untying the parachute harness. As he did so, he wondered what he should do about the parachute. Neither Professor Thomas nor Mr. West had suggested anything.

Billy shrugged. Right now he was glad he had it. It was at least four more hours until dawn, and it was a little colder than he thought it would be. He could use the parachute as a blanket. A little sleep wouldn't hurt him, either. In the morning he would leave the parachute out here on the desert ground, and walk on into town.

Billy lay down on the canopy, then rolled it around him like a cocoon. He was asleep within moments.

High overhead, unseen now by anyone, the big, black balloon drifted on a swiftly-moving current of air, north by northeast as it returned to Phoenix.

Billy was awakened by something wet. When he opened his eyes it was daylight, and he was being licked in the face by a curious, and fortunately friendly, dog. For a moment he was confused to find himself lying in the middle of nowhere, but the confusion passed quickly when he remembered what he had done last night.

"Good morning, dog," Billy said. He sat up and stretched. "Thanks for waking me up."

Billy started walking toward town. The easy part, jumping from a balloon that was two miles high, was done. Now came the hard part. He had to find Artemis Gordon.

The hired man at Spengler's Tobacco Shop came out onto the front porch carrying a bucket of water, soap, and wash clothes. He began washing the front windows, doing so with slow, methodical sweeps.

The hired man had also brought a broom and mop with him. When he finished with the windows he would sweep, then mop the porch. He was a very efficient hired man, and a particularly good bargain for the Spenglers, since they paid him no salary.

As Artie had told Fancy, there often came times when you had to trust someone. One such time was now, and upon the recommendation of Fancy, whose recommendation was seconded by Amber, Artemis Gordon put his trust, and his fate, in the hands of Clem and Sally Spengler.

As it turned out, it was a little easier for him to trust them than it was for them to trust him.

"No," Sally said, when Fancy and Amber had asked if they would hide Artemis Gordon. "Absolutely not. Cosgrove's men have searched our place a dozen times already, looking for him. And I know they are going to search it a dozen times more. What do you think would happen to us if they found him here?"

"Sally, never before have I turned my back on a fellow creature who needed help, and I'm not going to do it now,'' Clem argued.

"Clem, this isn't some hungry saddle bum, or a beaver with a thorn in its paw. This Artemis Gordon person is a wanted man."

"He's not really a wanted man," Clem said. "You heard what Amber and Fancy both said. He's a Secret Service agent, a federal lawman."

"He may not be a wanted man on the outside, but he is a wanted man in this town, and right now that's all that matters," Sally said.

"No, Sally. What matters is that he has come to help us—and now *he* needs help. I intend to help him."

Clem's insistence closed the argument. And though Sally had been in constant fear of discovery from the moment that Artie had arrived to take up his duties as handyman, it turned out that she had nothing to fear. As Sally had predicted, searchers came through at least another half a dozen times. But each time, they pushed by the new handyman the Spenglers had hired as if he were dirt—and in their eyes, he was.

For his end of the bargain, Artie really was working for them, doing as much as he could to help out. No one had told him to wash the windows and sweep and mop the front porch, but Artie could see that it was needed, so he took on the task. The fact that Artie was actually working helped to render him invisible. He had learned long ago that certain ubiquitous people, such as waiters, railroad porters, baggage handlers, and hostlers, tended to disappear. And as far as Cosgrove was concerned, that is exactly what he had done.

It was still very early in the morning when Artemis began his work. Only the truly employed were awake at this hour, such as the stable hands down at the livery barn; the blacksmith, whose ringing hammer blows at the anvil could already be heard all over town; and a couple of women who were talking to each other as they hung out their wash.

Cosgrove and his men were night owls. When the truly employed men and women of Presidio were going to sleep the previous night, Cosgrove, his men, and the women who provided their play were just getting started. They had a long night ahead of them, drinking, dancing, and finding other ways to entertain themselves.

This morning the roles were reversed. Cosgrove and his kind were still in their beds. Most of them would remain there until the sun was nearly straight overhead. The only exception to that was the armed men who worked in shifts guarding the pass, keeping outsiders out and insiders in.

When Billy walked by the church, which was the western-most building in town, Artie was the only one who happened to see him. The idea of someone coming into town from that direction made him curious. He knew there was nothing out there but desert. Where had he been? And why? Artie stopped mopping the porch for a moment as he stared.

When Billy got close enough, Artie recognized him. He didn't know him by name, but he knew this was the boy who delivered messages back in Phoenix.

Now his curiosity was really piqued. What was the Phoenix messenger boy doing here? Surely he wasn't delivering a message. All messages in and out of Presidio were very carefully controlled by Cosgrove.

On the other hand, there was a possibility that the boy could be bringing a message from Jim. He had no idea how he had gotten here, or why he was walking in from the desert—but he knew Jim well enough to know that Jim could come up with some pretty creative ways to get word to him. Was this one of those ways?

There was only one way to find out. Picking up the bucket, Artemis started walking toward the boy.

Billy watched the old man shuffling toward him, carrying the bucket. Where he was going with the bucket, Billy had no idea; but an old man with a bucket didn't seem particularly frightening to him. Nevertheless, he kept a wary eye on him.

Artie was studying Billy as carefully as Billy was studying him. The difference was, Billy's study was crude and obvious, whereas Artie was able to give the illusion of complete disinterest. He wasn't disinterested, though. He was very interested, especially when he saw Jim West's diamond stickpin in the boy's lapel.

"Where'd you get that stickpin, boy?" Artemis asked as the two came closer together.

Billy put his hand, quickly, over the pin.

"It ain't none of your concern, Mister, where I got it," he said. Was the man about to make a grab for it? This obviously wasn't the man he was looking for. This was an old, down-on-his-luck handyman, hardly the kind of person who would be working for the Secret Service.

"It is my concern if it belongs to my friend Jim West," Artie replied. "I'll be wanting to know how you came by it."

Startled by the mention of Jim West's name, Billy stared hard at the old man. This old window washer and stable-cleaner couldn't possibly be an agent from the Secret Service. And yet, he had recognized the stickpin just as Mr. West said he would, and he had called Jim West by name.

"Did Jim send you? Do you have anything for me?" Artie asked.

Billy shook his head. "You can't be the one I'm lookin' for," he said.

"Son, if you've got something for me, speak up. Don't let the looks fool you," Artie said.

Billy remembered then that Mr. West had told him that Artemis Gordon was a master of disguise. But surely, this was more than a disguise. He could see actual wrinkles in the man's face. Still, he had recognized the pin, and he did know about Jim West.

"Are you . . ." Billy started to ask, then he stopped. If this wasn't Artemis Gordon, even by merely asking the question, he might be putting the real Artemis Gordon in danger.

"I am Artemis Gordon," Artie said, intuitively aware that Billy would be hesitant to say the name first.

Billy shook his head. "You can't be," he said.

"Oh, but I am. How else would I have known about that stickpin?"

"I don't know," Billy answered.

"Did Jim give you any hints on how to recognize me?"

Suddenly remembering about the bottle of brandy, Billy smiled.

"Yes. He told me to ask you how much you paid for the—"

Artie groaned. "Not the brandy again," he interrupted. "Can't he come up with anything more original than that? That's about the third time he's used that. You know what I think? I think he is jealous. I think he is jealous because I know a good Napoleon brandy when I see it, and I am not afraid to spend good money to buy it.''

"How much?" Billy asked.

"One hundred dollars," Artie said. He stared hard at Billy. "At least that's the answer he expects me to give you. But you are obviously a young man who can keep a secret, so I will tell you the truth. I actually paid twice that much. I just didn't tell him because I would never hear the end of it.''

"Two hundred dollars?" Billy gasped.

"And worth every penny of it. My boy, a good brandy is, truly, the nectar of the gods. Now, tell me, how in the Sam Hill did you get here?''

"By parachute," Billy replied.

"What?"

"Parachute. It's like a giant umbrella that—" Billy started to explain, but Artie held up his hand, cutting him off.

"I know what a parachute is," he said. "But even with a parachute, you had to come from somewhere. Where? The top of a mountain?''

Billy pointed up. "From a balloon, last night," he said. "Mr. West and Professor Thomas brought me here.''

Artie laughed. "A balloon? You don't say. Well, leave it to my partner to come up with something original. Did you bring anything for me? A letter, perhaps?''

"No, sir, he didn't give me no letter, Mr. Gordon. Just a message," Billy said. He cleared his throat. "Mr. West wants me to tell you that he is coming over with the balloon again tonight. Only tonight, he's going to land the balloon and rescue Miss Morris. You're to be ready.''

"What's your name?'' Artie asked.

"Billy, sir. Billy Bates.''

"Well, Billy, I will be ready, thanks to you.''

19

When Jim showed up at Phoenix Park that night, he was driving a rented buckboard. In back of the buckboard were two large, heavy bags. He lifted them over the edge of the basket, then dropped them down inside.

"How heavy are those bags?" Professor Thomas asked.

"About one hundred pounds each," Jim said.

Thomas nodded. "And you will be taking them with you when you get off?"

"Yes."

"Good, good. That's two hundred pounds, plus your 165 weight, so we will be losing 365 pounds. The boy weighs about 125, and Miss Morris about 110. That's a net gain of 130 pounds. If I jettison another two hundred pounds in ballast, I should be able not only to get aloft, but also to have enough flexibility with the lifting gas and remaining ballast to navigate back to Phoenix."

"I'll leave that up to you," Jim said.

Professor Thomas stroked his chin for a moment, as if deep in thought.

"Mr. West, there is a way I can guarantee enough lifting gas for us to make the voyage," he said. "But it is more dangerous. I wouldn't want to do it without your knowledge and approval."

"What way is that?" Jim asked.

"All previous flights have been made with methane gas, what people call 'coal gas.' For this flight, I would propose that we use pure hydrogen. Hydrogen is so much lighter that it would give us half again the buoyancy. If we do that, there will be no problem in maintaining enough lift to launch again after we land, even though I will have vented it quite liberally."

"Isn't hydrogen flammable?"

"Yes, extremely so," Thomas replied. "So much so that most balloonists quit using it long ago. That's why I said it would be very dangerous, and why I said I would want your approval to use it. The slightest spark could cause a fire, and that would mean our immediate destruction."

"But it is more buoyant?"

"Much more buoyant," Thomas said.

"Then the risk is worth the result. Use hydrogen," Jim said.

Thomas smiled. "I was pretty sure you would go along with it. We are half-inflated now—with hydrogen."

In the Estrella valley, approximately one mile west of Presidio, Artemis Gordon, no longer in disguise, waited with Billy and Amber Morris. On the ground in front of them, Artie had lain out an X shape, made of small coal-oil pots. These were now burning, providing a marker beacon for the approaching balloon to use.

They had been waiting for over two hours now, and Amber, growing anxious that perhaps they wouldn't be here, searched the night sky in vain.

"No sense in lookin' up, Miss Morris," Billy said. "You can't hear it, and you wouldn't be able to see it even if it was right over you. The balloon is black and it just plumb disappears in the night."

"Billy, put out the pots," Artie suddenly said, drawing his pistol. "Miss Morris, get down. Someone is coming."

The flames were extinguished and the area was plunged into darkness. Amber and Billy knelt down behind some shrubbery.

"Really, Artie, did you think we could just land right on the spot, like parking a wagon?" Jim's voice called from some distance away.

Artie laughed out loud and put his pistol back in his holster. A moment later, Jim appeared out of the darkness. The two men met with a hearty handshake.

"I just wanted you to know where we were," Artie replied.

"Well, it was a good idea. And the balloon isn't too far from here. We were able to put it down about one mile south, I'd say." Jim looked at Billy, and smiled broadly. "I see you made it, Billy."

"He sure did," Artie replied. "This is one of the most courageous young men I have ever met."

"I agree with you," Jim said. "Is Miss Morris with you?"

"I'm right here," Amber said, standing up. "How is my father?"

"Your father is fine. And he's going to be much better tomorrow, when you get back."

"Is Billy right?" Amber asked. "We are flying back in a balloon?"

"Yes. Professor Thomas is waiting for us now. We have to get back as quickly as we can. Otherwise, we won't be able to get off the ground. I understand that, over a period of time, the gas begins to seep out."

"You'll love it, Miss Morris," Billy said. "It's great fun. You won't be afraid."

Amber smiled at Billy. "I'm not as courageous as you are," she said. "I will be afraid—but that won't stop me from doing it. I'll just close my eyes and hang on."

Twenty minutes later, the little party reached the balloon. It loomed huge and black against the night sky. It was held down by ballast, and secured down by half a dozen ropes. Professor Thomas was pacing about nervously, awaiting their return.

"We must hurry," Thomas said. "The gas leakage has been faster than I thought it would be. I don't know how much buoyancy we will have left."

Jim and Artie helped Amber into the gondola, then Billy climbed in as well. Professor Thomas followed, then the bags were handed out. The ropes were cut and ballast bags were dropped.

"Oh!" Amber said, startled as the balloon started up.

"Hallelujah!" Thomas called out. "We have enough buoyancy. We are aloft!"

"Oh," Amber exclaimed again, but this time her

voice came from high above as the balloon was ascending quickly.

"Bye, Mr. West, Mr. Gordon! Good luck!" Billy shouted. Already the black balloon had disappeared into the night.

"Mr. West, Mr. Gordon, the sun is up," Clem Spengler said. Clem was standing in the narthex of the church, looking out across the town square. Behind him, in the nave, the pews were filled with the men and women of the town. The children were asleep on pallets laid out in the sacristy and the chancel. Nearly the entire population of Presidio had been quietly awakened in the middle of the night, then brought to the church.

Cosgrove and his men were asleep in rooms on the second floor of the Last Chance Saloon. Not all had gone to bed alone, but Fancy had managed to get all of the soiled doves out this morning.

Nathan Algood owned the saloon, but he didn't stay there. He had a house on the west end of town. There had been some discussion as to whether or not Algood should be awakened and brought into the safety of the church as well, but it was decided to leave him out of it. There were some who feared that if Algood knew something was afoot, he would warn Cosgrove. They didn't exactly put him in the same category as Cosgrove, but neither did they count him as one of their own.

With the citizens of the town safely out of harm's way, Jim and Artie moved down to the other end of town to take up a position on the roof of the hardware store. The hardware store was directly across the street from the saloon, thus providing them with an unrestricted field of fire and visibility. It was in a manner of speaking, the "high ground".

Jim had brought the sawed-off Gatling gun that he had used with such effect when Tyson had attempted to rob his train. Though it had been hand-held when he had fired it that time, it was now mounted, and moved into position at one end of the roof. At the other end of the roof was a small, breach-loading Hotchkiss Cannon. The Hotchkiss, if expertly handled, was capable of firing twenty explosive shells per minute.

Jim had also brought an assortment of rockets and flash bombs, designed primarily to make a great deal of noise and light. These, he hoped, would spread so much confusion among Cosgrove's men that they wouldn't even be able to ascertain what was happening to them, let alone mount an effective resistance. The flash bombs and sound bombs looked like billiard balls. The flash bombs were white; the sound bombs black.

When all was ready, Artie picked up a black ball, and Jim a white. Nodding at each other, they pulled a small lanyard to activate the fuse, then threw the balls across the street toward the saloon. There was a faint double-crash of glass as the two bombs sailed in through closed windows.

Five seconds later there was a brilliant flash on the upper floor of the saloon, so bright that it could be seen through every window. That was followed almost immediately by a loud whistle, then a heavy booming sound. By then, two more bombs had been thrown and, immediately after them, two more.

The effect on the outlaws was immediate. Dazed and disoriented, they began running around on the top floor, most of them naked, or nearly so. They shouted in confusion and fear, and a few of them started firing out the windows, though they had no idea who they were supposed to be shooting at.

Jim hurried to the Gatling gun then, and began turning the crank. The gun roared as flames winked rapidly from the spinning barrels. Across the street he could see the bullets from his gun crashing through the windows, and poking holes in the side of the building. He swung the gun back and forth, maintaining a steady stream of firing, as if squirting water from a hose.

As Jim worked the Gatling gun, Artie manned the Hotchkiss. Jim had been restricted by weight as to just how many of the Hotchkiss rounds he could bring, but there were at least forty, and Artie was slamming them into the breach, firing, then snapping open the breach to eject the empty shell casing so he could fire the next one. He was putting out one shell every five seconds, and they were exploding in the saloon with devastating effect. Jim saw one hit the chimney just where it joined the roof. The chimney was blown apart, sending out a shower of broken brick and jagged bits of mortar.

A few of Cosgrove's men determined where all the shooting was coming from and they tried to return fire, but the effort was weak. One minute earlier they had been asleep in their beds, more than half of them sleeping off a hangover. Now they were fighting for their lives against a mostly unseen enemy, and they were doing so without benefit of leadership, because Cosgrove had been strangely quiet from the moment the shooting had begun.

"Artie," Jim called across the roof to his friend. "Artie, cease fire."

Artie stopped firing and both the Hotchkiss and the

Gatling grew quiet. For several seconds the echoes of the battle came back from the mountain walls, then they too, subsided, and a deathly silence fell across the town.

Jim waited, keeping his eyes on the saloon across the street, studying every window, studying too the doors, and the open space between the saloon and the buildings to either side. Those open spaces gave him a view of the alley and he wanted to make certain no one was getting away that way.

"Cosgrove!" Jim shouted.

"He ain't here!" a voice replied.

"Where is he?" Jim asked.

"How are we supposed to know where he is?"

"Come out onto the porch with your hands up," Jim ordered. "All of you."

"We ain't none of us fool enough to do that. If you want us, you're going to have to come get us."

Jim nodded at Artie. Artie let loose another shell, and Jim opened fire with the Gatling gun again. They kept up a sustained fire for about ten seconds. Someone stuck a broom handle out one of the upstairs windows. A white flag was attached to it. Jim signaled to Artie and they stopped firing.

When the echoes died and it was silent once more, Jim called out to the outlaws.

"Are you coming out now? Or do you want to play some more?" he asked.

"No, no, we're comin' out. Don't do no more shootin'," the voice from the saloon called.

A minute later the batwing doors opened and a man, carrying the broom with the white flag, stepped out onto the porch.

"Come all the way out, so that you are standing in

the middle of the street," Jim ordered. "And keep your hands up."

Nervously, the man did as Jim directed.

"Where are the others?" Artie asked.

"We're comin', we're comin'," a voice called back. A few seconds later the front door of the saloon opened and nearly a dozen men, in various stages of dress from long underwear to fully dressed, came outside. Holding their hands over their heads and looking around in shock as if unable to understand what had just happened to them, they filed into the middle of the street, to join the first man.

"Keep them covered, Artie. I'm going down," Jim said. Hurrying downstairs, Jim stepped out into the middle of the group. By now others from the town were coming, cautiously, out into the street. There was a sense of awakening, of new freedom about the townspeople, and they were almost giddy as they talked to each other in low but excited tones, pointing to the men who had held them captive for so long.

"They don't look like much now, do they?"

"Ha. Look at them skinny legs. Without their guns, they're plum puny-lookin'."

"Where's Cosgrove? I don't see Cosgrove."

"Help!" a woman screamed, and Jim and the townspeople who had gathered in front of the saloon looked toward the other end of the street, in the direction of the scream.

Cosgrove was standing there, in the middle of the street, with his left arm around Fancy's neck. In his right hand was a pistol, and the barrel of the pistol was pressed against Fancy's temple.

"You people lookin' for me?"

"It's Cosgrove! He's got Fancy!" someone said.

"Drago . . . or whatever your name is," Cosgrove shouted to Artie. "You push those two fancy weapons you got up there on the roof with you, over the side."

Artie paused for a moment, and Cosgrove cocked his pistol. Fancy let out a little whimper.

"Do it now!" Cosgrove ordered.

"Go ahead, Artie," Jim said.

Artie pushed the two weapons over the side.

"Okay, boys, get your guns back," Cosgrove said. "We're takin' over again."

As Cosgrove spoke, he took his gun away from Fancy's head and used it to wave. When he did, Fancy bit him hard, on the arm. He let out a shout of pain and let her go as he examined his now-bleeding arm. Fancy dashed toward one of the buildings, and Cosgrove aimed at her.

"No, Cosgrove!" Jim shouted.

Cosgrove turned back toward Jim and fired. The bullet whizzed by Jim's ear, hit the dirt behind him, then skipped off with a high-pitched whine.

For the moment, Jim couldn't shoot back because Fancy was still in the line of fire. Cosgrove, realizing that, smiled, and fired again. Jim dropped, then rolled. As he rolled, he saw one of the outlaws starting toward the Gatling gun. He shot at the Gatling gun, hitting it just in front of the outlaw and causing the outlaw to jump back.

"Artie, keep them covered!" Jim shouted. "The rest of you, get down!"

When Jim looked back toward Cosgrove, he saw him diving behind a watering trough. Jim threw a bullet in his direction and saw the water splash, just as Cosgrove got down and out of sight.

Jim got up and sprinted toward the opposite side of the street, then knelt down behind a porch. He looked over at the watering trough, trying to find an opening for a shot.

A flash of light from the morning sun caught him in the eyes. For a moment he was confused because the sun was behind him. Then, when he looked toward the source of the light, he saw that it was a mirror. The mirror was in the window of a dressmaker's shop, and it was being held by Fancy. She twisted the mirror and the flash of light went away, to be replaced by the reflection of Cosgrove.

"Bless you, girl," Jim said under his breath. Fancy was turning the mirror so that he could see exactly what Cosgrove was doing.

The outlaw was inching along on his belly to the far end of the watering trough. Jim took slow and deliberate aim at the end of the trough where he knew Cosgrove's head would appear.

Slowly, Cosgrove peered around the corner of the trough to see where Jim was, and what was going on. Jim cocked his pistol and waited. When enough of Cosgrove's body was exposed to give him a target, Jim squeezed the trigger.

Half an hour later the prisoners, including those who had been standing guard in the pass, were safely locked up in the newly activated Presidio jail. Jim and Artie rode by the hardware store on their way out of town. Propped up in front of the hardware store were four one-by-eight-foot boards, and tied to those boards were four bodies: Cosgrove, Tyson, Kitridge, and Spivey. The undertaker, bowing to modesty, had clothed the men. It was good that he did, because a crowd of nearly one hundred was gathered in front of the store, gawking at the bodies. Magnesium powder flared as the two Secret Service agents rode by, and though Jim thought someone was getting a picture of the bodies, the camera was aimed, instead, at them.

By mid-afternoon a blown-up photograph of two men, riding away so that their faces weren't visible, would be displayed in the front window of McCorkle's Photo Gallery. A sign under the picture would say, simply:

TO THESE TWO MEN,
WE OWE OUR THANKS.
THE MEN AND WOMEN OF
PRESIDIO, A. T.

The private train was assembled and the engine had its steam pressure up. All the good-byes had been said, and Jim and Artie saw to it that Billy Bates and Professor Thomas received the accolades due them. They were about to leave, when there was a knock at the door of the car.

When Artie opened the door, Billy handed him a package.

"Compliments of the governor, sir," Billy said.

"Billy," Jim called from within the car. "Back to your old job, I see."

"Old job nothin'," Billy answered. "I'm the governor's page. You know what that is?"

"Yes, I know. It is a very important job," Jim said.

"I didn't know what it was until the governor told me. He said it would be good training for when I become a Secret Service agent, like you and Mr. Gordon."

"It will be," Jim said.

"Well, I've got to be going now," Billy said. "Us pages are busy people."

Billy hopped down from the train just as the engineer blew his whistle to signal that they were getting under way.

"What did the governor send?" Jim asked.

Artie opened the box and took out a bottle of brandy. There was a letter with it.

Dear Mr. West and Mr. Gordon,

I was told of your taste for fine brandy. I hope you find this bottle to your taste. It is a bottle from the personal wine cellar of George Washington. Take it, with my sincere thanks for all that you did for my daughter, for me, and for the territory of Arizona.

"What a wonderful thing for the governor to do," Artie said. He began looking around the car. "Where is the corkscrew?"

Jim took the bottle from him. "What do you mean, where is the corkscrew? We aren't going to open this."

"What?"

"This is much too fine a bottle to be opened and consumed like a jug of barroom whiskey. No, sir. We are going to keep this on permanent display."

"A heathen," Artie said, slapping his hand to his head in consternation. "Lord help me, my partner is a heathen."

The train gathered speed as it passed by Phoenix Park where, once again, Professor Thomas was preparing for an aerostation.